CHAPTER ONE

Faith slipped the dress over her head and examined herself in her bedroom mirror. The shapeless shift dress was a dull shade of blue and went down past her knees. She frowned. She looked reliable. Responsible. That was what she was going for. But she didn't look like herself.

She pulled off the dress and tossed it onto her bed, then began flipping through her closet again. Surely she had something less frumpy that still looked professional. She needed to make a good first impression.

Faith glanced at the alarm clock on her nightstand. She only had five minutes until she had to leave for her job interview. She had a good feeling about this job. She'd been searching for a stable nanny position for months now. Over the past year, she'd had jobs on and off, but none of them had lasted. She'd had to deal with entitled brats, parents who treated her like a servant, or worse, parents who expected her to single-handedly raise their children.

However, this job sounded promising. A family she'd

worked for in the past had recommended her to a friend of theirs, a divorcee named Eve. Faith didn't know much about her, other than the fact that she had twins, a boy and a girl. The address she'd been given was in an upper-class suburb so the family had to be outrageously rich. In Faith's experience that usually meant spoiled kids and detached parents, but Faith was staying positive.

She pulled a blouse from her closet and held it up before her. It was white with a contrasting black collar. She slipped it on, along with a black A-line skirt, and inspected herself in the mirror again.

It was an improvement on the dress, although it was a little drab for Faith's tastes. For most of her life, she'd been forced to dress conservatively. Now that she was free to experiment, her tastes were on the wilder side. From her clothes to her hair, her appearance was ever-changing. Over the years, she'd dyed her hair every color imaginable, from black to bright pink.

But for now she'd gone back to a natural-looking light brown. The kind of people wealthy enough to hire someone to take care of their kids full-time didn't want pink-haired nannies. They wanted only the most respectable, dependable people to watch over their little angels.

Her cell phone buzzed. She dug it out from under the pile of clothes on her bed. It was a message from her friend Lindsey.

Good luck with the interview! Let me know how it goes.

Faith shot Lindsey a reply and picked up her purse, tucking her phone away in it. It was time to get going. She paused by her dresser, then grabbed her favorite lipstick

FREEING HER

ANNA STONE

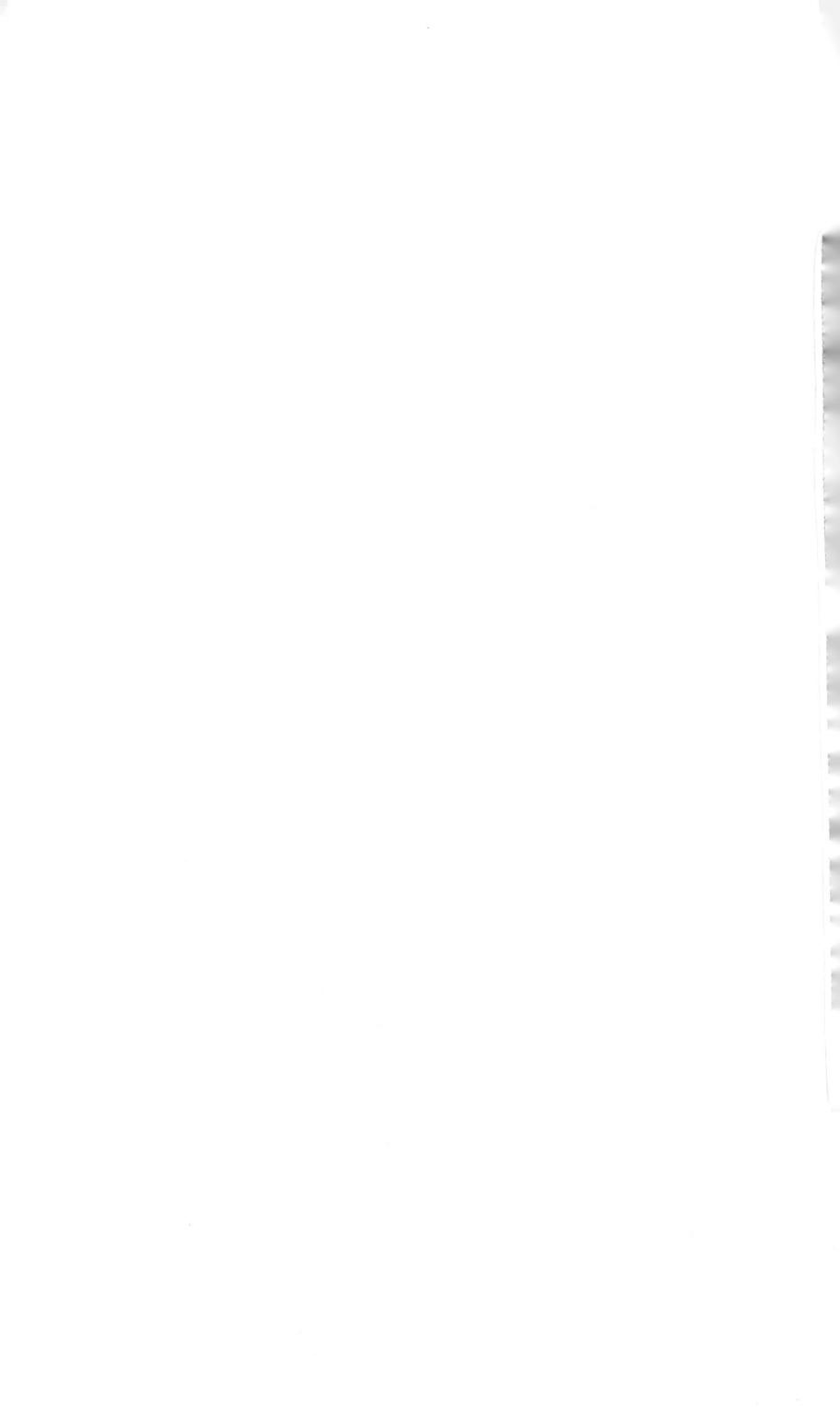

© 2019 Anna Stone

All rights reserved. No part of this publication may be replicated, reproduced, or redistributed in any form without the prior written consent of the publisher.

This is a work of fiction. Names, characters, places, and incidents either are the products of the author's imagination or are used fictitiously. Any resemblance to actual persons, living or dead, businesses, companies, events, or locales is entirely coincidental.

Cover by Kasmit Covers

ISBN: 9780648419259

and swiped it across her lips, turning them a warm shade of red.

She smiled into the mirror. *That's better.*

Faith rang Eve's doorbell. She'd never been to this part of the city before. All the houses were multistory mansions, with photo-perfect gardens and expensive cars parked in the driveways. But the house she stood before, a three-story mansion at the end of a quiet cul-de-sac, was the grandest of them all.

The front door opened. A tall, blonde woman stood in the doorway, her deep hazel eyes hidden behind a pair of stylish tortoiseshell rimmed glasses. She looked to be in her early thirties.

The woman gave her a tight smile. "You must be Faith."

"Yes," Faith said. "Hi."

"Eve." The woman stepped to the side and gestured into the house. "Why don't you come in?"

Faith followed Eve inside, Eve's heels clicking on the marble floor with each step. Faith examined her as they walked. She was beautiful in an understated way. Despite her slender, willowy frame, her confident manner made it clear that she was anything but delicate. She wore a light-gray, structured knee-length dress that subtly enhanced her shape. Her hair was curly, but not like Faith's, which hung in loose, wild waves, no matter what she did with it. Eve's curls were neatly arranged in a short bob style that reminded Faith of a vintage pin-up model. Although the look could have used some color, Eve exuded a sense of style, which was something Faith had always found attractive in a person.

Not that Faith was thinking about her potential boss that way.

Faith peered around her as they walked down the hall. There were an endless number of rooms, all lavishly decorated. It wasn't surprising. Only the wealthiest of families could afford full-time nannies. But this house was like nothing Faith had ever seen. With its pristine white walls, marble floors, and elaborate decor, it was a palace in the middle of suburbia.

However, there was something off about it. Something missing. Faith realized what it was when Eve directed her into a lounge room. The house was too quiet. Too neat and organized. There were no signs that children lived here at all.

Eve gestured toward an armchair. "Take a seat."

Faith sat down. Eve sat in the couch across from her, folding her hands on her lap in a ladylike manner. She looked Faith up and down, appraising her. Her eyes narrowed at Faith's bright red lipstick.

Faith shifted in her seat.

"So, Faith," Eve said. "Tell me about yourself."

"Well, I've been babysitting my whole life," Faith began. "I had a huge family, and I used to take care of my younger brothers and sisters and all my cousins growing up. Then I did some babysitting in college, and when I graduated I started nannying full-time."

It wasn't what she'd planned to do after college. She'd attended art school, mostly because she'd had no idea what she wanted to do with her life, and when she'd finished she'd struggled to find a job. So, when one of the families she babysat for had offered her a nanny position, she'd snapped it up. She enjoyed it, after all. And she was good at it. "I've worked for a few families long-term. The Yangs were the last."

"They spoke highly of you. So did your references. And your qualifications all checked out. I also took the liberty of doing a thorough background check. It came up clean."

That was a relief. Faith was always worried that anyone who dug around in her background would find out about the brief period she went 'missing' eight years ago, but it hadn't come up yet. Perhaps it was because she'd been a minor at the time.

"I'm going to be frank," Eve said. "I'm in desperate need of a nanny. I returned to work recently for the first time since the twins were born. I was in marketing before I had the children so I decided to start my own small firm. But it's becoming impossible to keep up with work while looking after the twins' needs. For now, I share custody with their father, but most of the real work falls on me."

Eve crossed her stockinged legs and smoothed down her skirt. "I'm looking for someone to help out with the more practical parts of taking care of the twins. Taking them to lessons, chores, and so on. We have housekeepers for general household tasks, and I won't expect you to do anything that will get in the way of your duties with the children. But I may need you to do the odd personal errand for me. You'll be well compensated, of course."

"That's fine with me." The last family Faith had worked for briefly had had her scrubbing toilets, so this would be an improvement.

"Can you drive?" Eve asked.

"Yes."

"I'll supply you with a car to travel to and from work, and to drive the kids around. We used to use a car service, but I decided to cut down on some of our unnecessary expenses. Live more modestly."

Faith glanced around. This was living modestly? What had Eve been living like before?

"I'll need you to stay overnight on occasion," Eve said. "I'll have one of the spare rooms set aside for your use. And you're not to bring anyone else around the kids. Friends. Partners."

"I would never do anything like that."

"You'd be surprised how many babysitters I've had that think it's appropriate."

Faith studied Eve. For the past few minutes, she'd felt an air of discomfort coming from the other woman. Faith had just thought it was because Eve was uptight. But perhaps Eve was simply feeling uneasy about the idea of leaving her children in a stranger's hands.

"I'm no babysitter," Faith said. "I'm a professional. I might seem young, but I'm fully qualified, and I've been looking after children my entire life. I assure you, your kids will be in capable hands with me."

"And I expect nothing less." Almost imperceptibly, Eve seemed to relax. "Now, your hours will be erratic for now. Since my ex-husband and I don't have a custody agreement yet, the days I have the twins vary, but I'll make sure you get plenty of time off. Speaking of the twins, why don't I call them down so you can meet them? They're upstairs."

"Sure," Faith said.

Eve went out into the hall. "Leah? Ethan? Come down here, please."

Faith waited in silence. She heard the patter of feet coming down the stairs.

"No running, you two," Eve said.

The footsteps slowed. Moments later, Eve walked back into the room accompanied by two small children: a girl and a boy. They had their mother's blonde hair, carefully combed and styled, and the same hazel eyes, not to mention the same serious expressions. They were dressed as though they'd walked right out of an upmarket children's clothing catalog.

"Leah, Ethan, this is Faith." Eve sat them down on the couch and perched on the arm of it next to them. "Why don't you introduce yourselves?"

The children did as they were told. They were polite and well-spoken. Faith questioned them about school and their interests. They were both involved in half a dozen extracurricular activities.

"As you can see, Leah and Ethan have plenty on their plates," Eve said. "They're in first grade now, and they're getting extra tutoring. They both take Spanish and French lessons, as well as music classes. Piano for Ethan and violin for Leah. Leah does ballet, and Ethan plays baseball and soccer. That's on top of all their scheduled play dates and other social activities."

Scheduled play dates? Spanish *and* French? It was a lot for a pair of seven-year-olds. Faith had worked for parents like Eve before, who filled every moment of their children's days with activities and micromanaged their lives, but this seemed excessive.

"Now, house rules," Eve continued. "We keep screen time to a minimum unless necessary for schoolwork. There are no TVs in the house. And no junk food. Preparing breakfast and snacks will be your responsibility."

As Eve continued, Faith tried her best to keep her mind from wandering. Eve had a long list of rules. Faith glanced at the twins, sitting quietly beside Eve. They were extremely well-mannered for their age. Probably because of their mother.

Eve rested her hand on Leah's shoulder. "That's about everything. I have high expectations of anyone who works for me, but I'm offering a generous salary, plus benefits. Health insurance, dental, paid leave."

"Sounds great," Faith said.

"Then you can start tomorrow."

Faith blinked. That was it? "Sure." Everything about the job sounded perfect. The only thing she was uncertain of was how well she'd get along with Eve.

"The job is yours," Eve said. "All that's left to discuss is your salary."

"Right." Faith had been so thrown by the job offer that she hadn't thought about negotiating pay first.

But when Eve gave her a figure, it was far higher than anything Faith would have asked for. Eve wasn't kidding about offering a generous salary. Unease stirred within her.

Just how much did Eve expect from Faith in return?

After a brief discussion about Faith's duties, Eve sent Leah and Ethan back upstairs. "I have to get the twins to school. That will be your job from now on. I need you here at seven in the morning tomorrow to wake them up and get them ready."

Faith nodded. "I'll be here."

Eve ushered her to the door and said a polite farewell. Faith walked down the path cutting across the manicured lawn and onto the sidewalk. As soon as she was out of sight of the house, she skipped a couple of steps and pulled out her phone to call Lindsey.

Her friend answered after a couple of rings. "How did the interview go?"

Faith grinned. "I got the job."

"That's great! Let's hope it's better than the last one."

"I already know it's going to be. I have a good feeling about this."

But as she walked down the sidewalk, Faith remembered Eve's disapproving eyes on her red lips. The proper, buttoned-up woman was her complete opposite.

But Faith would make it work.

CHAPTER TWO

Faith shepherded the twins downstairs for breakfast. Both were dressed immaculately in tiny blazers and ties, the uniform of their exclusive private school. Faith had ironed them to Eve's specifications the evening before.

She'd been working for Eve for three days now. Her suspicions about her new boss had quickly been confirmed. She wasn't one of those rich parents who let 'the help' raise their kids. With Eve, Faith had the opposite problem. She could barely do anything without Eve looming over her, giving her instructions. Combined with the long workdays, the job was taxing. However, the twins were going to their father's in a few days, giving Faith three days off in a row. She was already looking forward to it.

She and the twins entered the dining room. Eve sat at the head of the table reading a newspaper, a cup of coffee in her hand. She was dressed for work in a pantsuit and cream-colored blouse.

"Good morning, sweethearts." Eve beckoned the twins

over and planted a kiss on each of their foreheads. She looked at Leah and plucked the brightly colored butterfly barrette out of her hair, scowling. "You're not wearing that to school."

"Faith said I could wear it," Leah whined.

"Faith doesn't know the school's dress code." Eve looked pointedly at Faith. "I'll send you a copy. And no more pigtails. It looks childish."

"Okay," Faith replied. It wasn't like Leah was a child or anything.

Leah sat down at the table and pouted. "Everyone else wears stuff like this."

"That doesn't matter," Eve said. "Rules are rules."

Faith served the twins their breakfast, a perfectly balanced meal she'd prepared as per Eve's instructions, then sat down and drank her coffee while the family ate breakfast. They chatted animatedly as they did. Even Eve seemed to perk up. Despite her strictness, she wasn't an uncaring parent. And despite the kids being absurdly well behaved, they seemed happy and healthy.

It made Faith miss her own family. She wondered what they were all up to. It had been a while since she'd heard from her sister. She was getting worried.

When the twins finished their breakfast, Eve sent them upstairs to brush their teeth. Faith began clearing the dishes from the table.

"Make sure you get the kids to school on time," Eve said. "When they were with Harrison last week, they were late two days in a row."

"I will." School didn't start for another forty-five minutes. They had plenty of time.

"And don't forget, they have Spanish lessons this afternoon."

"Okay." Faith had already memorized their schedules, which Eve had given her on day one. But she still insisted on laying everything out every single morning. She managed Faith just as much as she managed her kids.

It was frustrating, but Faith tried not to hold it against Eve. Eve was working full-time and almost single-handedly raising two kids. Faith didn't know what the situation was with her ex-husband, but it didn't sound like he was much help in that department.

"Now, I need you to run some errands for me," Eve said.

As Eve continued to list off instructions, she took off her glasses and wiped down the lenses. With her glasses off, Faith could see all the colors in Eve's eyes, a mesmerizing swirl of greens and browns.

What lay behind those eyes of hers? Eve's face was the kind that gave nothing away. Faith found it equal parts frustrating and intriguing. She was like a puzzle to be solved. Was there more to Eve than the proper, boring facade she presented?

Eve replaced her glasses on her nose, breaking the spell. She stood up. "I need to get to work. Call me if you need anything. And make sure everything I asked of you gets done."

Faith nodded. It was going to be a long day.

Faith opened the trunk of her shiny new car and grabbed the bags of groceries inside. She'd finally finished the long list of errands Eve had given her. She still had a few hours before she had to pick up the twins, but she had plenty to do around the house.

As she carried the groceries to the door, her phone rang. She put her bags down and picked up the phone. It was Eve.

"I need a favor," Eve said. "My pen leaked on my blouse. I have a meeting in a couple of hours. Can you bring me a fresh one?"

"Sure," Faith replied.

"Just choose something from my closet. My work clothes are on the left."

Faith took the groceries inside, packed everything in the fridge, then headed toward Eve's bedroom. It was at the back of the house, along with a set of rooms that Eve reserved for her use only. The twins weren't allowed in this part of the house, so Faith hadn't seen it yet.

As she walked down the hall, she saw that Eve's rooms were off-limits to the twins for a good reason. They were even more pristine than the rest of the house and filled with all kinds of valuable, breakable furniture and decor. There were a few pieces of art on the walls by artists whose style Faith recognized from her art school days.

She walked further down the hall, spotting a sun-filled office, a huge bathroom, and a small lounge room. At the end of the hall, she came to a bedroom. Eve's bedroom. It was as luxurious as all the other rooms, and it was just as neat. The large bed looked like it had never been slept on, the crisp white sheets on it pulled tight. Eve's walk-in closet was on the other side of the bed.

Faith tiptoed into the room, afraid to disturb anything. She entered the closet and turned on the light.

Wow. The closet was the size of Faith's entire bedroom. All around her were endless racks of clothes and shelves of shoes. There was a full-length mirror surrounded by lights and a mannequin on which a simple black dress hung. A small dressing table held an array of jewelry.

Faith walked around the room, examining everything. For someone as fashion-mad as Faith, this was heaven. Although most of Eve's clothes weren't to Faith's taste, everything was stylish and finely made. She reached for a woolen pea coat, stroking it gently. It was delightfully soft. She wondered what it would feel like on.

No. Focus. She walked over to the rack on the left. Just as Eve had told her, it held all work-appropriate clothes. There were a dozen near-identical cream and white blouses, as well as pantsuits and skirts in various shades of black and gray. Judging by how well everything Eve wore fit her, each item in the closet was tailor-made for Eve's body.

Not that Faith had noticed her boss's body.

She pulled out a blouse at random. It would go well with the pantsuit Eve had been wearing. She found an empty garment bag and slipped the blouse into it.

Out of the corner of her eye, she spotted something tucked away at the other end of the wardrobe. It was a bright blue sequined cocktail dress. And it was scandalously short.

Faith flipped through the pieces next to it. There were a few more cocktail dresses, most of them more modest than the blue one, as well as some evening gowns. One of them was a stunning piece, a long black dress with a structured bodice. On the floor beneath the dresses, almost hidden by the long skirts, were two pairs of stiletto heels with red soles.

Did Eve ever wear such sexy clothing? Faith pictured it in her mind. Eve in sequins and stilettos, those long legs of hers bared, the low cut of the dress showing off the shoulders and chest that Eve kept under button-up work shirts.

Faith shook her head. Her imagination was getting out of hand. Besides, those stilettos were covered in dust. It was clear that they were rarely ever worn.

Faith hopped in the elevator and pressed the button for the floor of Eve's office. She looked around. She was the only person in the elevator who wasn't wearing a suit. These stuffy men and women made Eve seem eccentric.

She got out at Eve's floor and was faced with a wide-open reception area. A bored-looking woman sat behind the reception desk. Faith caught her eye.

"Can I help you?" the woman asked.

"I'm here to see Eve," Faith said. "She asked me to drop something off."

"You must be Faith. Ms. Lincoln is expecting you." The woman stood up. "I'll take you to her. Come with me."

Faith followed the receptionist into the office. She looked around, wide-eyed. The office was huge and abuzz with activity. This was Eve's definition of a 'small' firm? And all this belonged to her? Faith had underestimated Eve. Given the draconian way she ran her home, Faith shouldn't have been surprised that Eve commanded all of this.

They reached a door with Eve's name on the nameplate. The receptionist knocked.

"Come in," Eve said from inside.

The receptionist opened the door and gestured Faith inside. Eve sat behind a desk, her eyes fixed on her laptop. The room was very similar to Eve's office at home.

"Thank you, Andrea," Eve said. "Shut the door, please."

Andrea closed the door, leaving the two of them alone.

"Faith, thank you for this." Eve continued to type away. "You're a lifesaver."

"It's no trouble," Faith said.

"I usually keep a spare in my office, but the kids got their hands all over it when they were here with me last week." Eve shut her laptop, stood up and rounded the desk. "Andrea keeps telling me to hire a personal assistant for these things, but I can't bring myself to trust someone else with important duties."

So Eve's control issues weren't just to do with Faith? That was good to know.

Eve took the blouse from Faith and set it down on the desk behind her, then pulled off her jacket, revealing an ink stain near the top of her shirt. "Don't go anywhere. You can take this to the dry cleaner for me. With luck, they can get the stain out."

"Sure," Faith said.

Without hesitation, Eve began unbuttoning her shirt. The top of her bra peeked out of it. It was lacy, red, and cut low.

Did Eve always wear such racy underwear under her clothes?

Eve's hands stopped at the next button. "Faith?"

"Huh?" Faith looked up. Eve was staring back at her through her tortoiseshell glasses, her eyes piercing.

"I said, am I making you uncomfortable?"

"No." Heat crept up Faith's face. "I'll just turn around."

Faith spun around. Behind her, she could hear the swish of clothing. She willed herself to not imagine Eve undressing. What was wrong with her? Just this morning, Faith had been thinking about how much Eve got on her nerves, and now this?

"I'm done," Eve said. "Here."

Faith turned around to face Eve. Eve tucked the bottom of her blouse into her pants and handed Faith the ink-stained shirt.

"Before you go." Eve leaned back against the front of her desk. "How are you finding the job so far? Any issues?"

"No," Faith said. "Leah and Ethan are easy kids."

"And everything else? I know I can be"—Eve pressed her lips together, searching for a word—"*demanding* at times."

"It's fine. I can handle it."

"Good. Let me know if anything comes up." Eve slid her jacket back on and went to sit behind her desk. "Thanks again, Faith."

Faith left Eve's office. She needed to get a grip. Eve was her boss. And even if she wasn't, she was not Faith's type at all.

So why couldn't Faith stop thinking about her?

CHAPTER THREE

Faith sat on the floor in the lounge room with the twins, waiting for Harrison to pick them up. They were going to stay with their father for a few days, which meant Faith would finally get some time off.

In the meantime, Faith was helping the twins with their homework. For every question they got right, Faith gave them a sticker. At some point, the twins had started sticking the stickers on each other's arms and faces, laughing as they did. Eve definitely wouldn't approve, but it kept the twins motivated, so Faith didn't stop them.

She glanced out into the hall. Eve was in the other room working. It seemed like Eve disapproved of everything Faith did. Even when she didn't say so, the dark look in her eyes spoke volumes. At least, Faith thought it was disapproval that she sensed. It was hard to tell what was going on in Eve's head.

Leah stuck a sticker on Faith's cheek and giggled. The doorbell rang.

"Faith?" Eve's voice rang out across the hall. "Can you get that, please? It's probably Harrison."

"Sure." Faith ruffled Ethan's hair and got up. "I'll be right back."

She headed down the hall and opened the front door. A well-dressed woman around Faith's age stood before her.

"Hi," the woman said. "I'm Harrison's assistant. He sent me to pick up Ethan and Lily."

"You mean Leah?" Faith asked.

"Right. That's what I meant. Harrison, he's in a meeting, but he'll be out soon."

Faith looked her up and down. "Let me go get Eve."

She headed back inside, and found Eve in the lounge room, removing the stickers from the twins' arms, an irritated expression on her face.

"Eve?" Faith said. "There's a woman at the door. She says she's Harrison's assistant."

Eve let out a hard sigh. "Tall, red hair, looks like she's just out of high school?"

"Uh, yes. She says she's here to pick up the twins."

"Harrison is supposed to pick them up himself."

"She said he's in a meeting."

"Of course he is." Eve adjusted the collar of Ethan's shirt, her irritation held back. "You've packed the kids' bags?"

Faith nodded. "They're by the door."

Eve addressed the twins. "It's time to go to your father's. Let's go."

Obediently, the twins got up and said goodbye to Faith. Eve shepherded them to the door.

Faith packed up the books and toys strewn around the room. Three whole days off. She was looking forward to it.

She'd made plans to catch up with friends, starting with dinner with Lindsey in a few hours. But mostly, she just wanted to put her feet up and relax.

Faith heard the front door slam shut, then the telltale click of Eve's heels on the floor in the hall.

"You sent your PA to pick up the kids again?" Eve's voice echoed through the empty house. "I don't care about your meeting. You knew you had to come get them this evening. You agreed to pick them up personally. You're lucky I let them go with her at all!"

Was Eve on the phone to Harrison? Faith tried her hardest not to eavesdrop, but it was impossible with Eve yelling as she was.

"You expect me to send my children off with some stranger?" There was a long pause. "That's different. A nanny is a professional, not someone who's barely qualified to get coffee, let alone work with children." Eve paused again. "Is that what your mother thinks? Last time I checked, she wasn't the one raising the twins."

Eve strolled past the lounge room and spotted Faith inside. Judging by the look on her face, she'd forgotten Faith was there.

"I have to go," Eve said. "Next time, pick them up yourself, or they're not going anywhere." She hung up the phone.

Faith made a show of busying herself putting away the kids' books.

"I suppose you heard all that?" Eve said.

"Er, just a little," Faith replied.

"I apologize for raising my voice. Things between Harrison and I can be strained at times."

"Sorry to hear that."

"Don't be. It's better than being married to him."

Silence hung over them. It was rare for the two of them to be alone in the house.

Eve looked at Faith's face. Her eyes slid down toward Faith's lips, her head tilting to the side. "Come here," she said.

Faith's heart began to race. She took a few steps forward, closer and closer to Eve. As soon as she was within reach, Eve lifted her hand toward Faith's face.

Faith's heart beat even faster. What was Eve doing?

Eve's fingertips brushed Faith's cheek. A shiver rolled down the back of Faith's neck. She'd never been this close to Eve before. She smelled faintly of flowers with a hint of spice, and her lips had a reddish tinge and an inviting fullness.

Eve pulled away and held up a little gold star. "You shouldn't let the kids treat you like a toy."

Faith blinked. *Right.* The sticker. Leah had put it there. "I... It's fine. I don't mind."

Eve gave her a slight smile. "They're lucky to have a nanny like you." She looked past Faith at the room beyond. "You've finished tidying up?"

"Yes," Faith stammered.

"You can go home now. I'll see you in a few days."

Faith mumbled a goodbye, grabbed her things, and left the room without looking back.

When Faith got home, she jumped straight into the shower. She had a couple of hours before she was due to meet

Lindsey for dinner. Faith was hoping to convince her to have drinks afterward. She needed to unwind.

She was looking forward to catching up with Lindsey. She was the closest thing Faith had to family these days. The two of them had been inseparable since their first day of art school when they met. They'd lived together for most of their time at college, and they'd stayed close even after they'd graduated a couple of years ago. But last year, Lindsey had moved in with her girlfriend Camilla, who lived just outside the city. Since then, she and Faith didn't get to spend as much time together as they used to. Faith missed her.

As she got out of the shower and dried herself off, her phone rang. She darted into her bedroom. Her phone was on the dresser, Lindsey's name flashing on the screen.

Faith picked it up. "Hi, Lindsey."

"Faith," Lindsey said. "I know we're supposed to have dinner tonight, but I just remembered I have plans with Camilla. We made them a month ago. I completely forgot."

"Oh. That's okay."

"I'm really sorry. I can't get out of this. It's with a bunch of Camilla's friends, and it's really rare that everyone is free at the same time."

"It's all right." Faith tried her best to hide her disappointment. "We can reschedule."

"Maybe we don't have to," Lindsey said. "You could always join us. I should warn you, we're going to Lilith's Den."

Faith frowned. "Isn't that a sex club?" Lindsey had mentioned it to Faith before. She and Camilla went occasionally. They had some kind of kinky relationship that Faith didn't quite understand.

"It's *not* a sex club. It's a BDSM club. There's a difference. And we're going there to hang out and catch up, that's all."

"Right," Faith said.

"Really. To tell you the truth, it's probably going to be boring. Whenever Camilla's friends get together, everyone just sits around talking about investments and whiskey. I could use some company. Plus, it's 'ladies only' night."

That was a definite plus. Faith liked women, men, and everyone in between, but she rarely dated men these days. It seemed like every guy she dated ended up being too hung up on traditional gender roles. They wanted Faith to be this dutiful, subservient, utterly ladylike girlfriend. She'd had enough of that in her life. She rarely had to worry about that when she dated women.

"That doesn't matter," she said. "I'm not looking to meet anyone at a place like *that*."

"Since when are you such a prude?" Lindsey teased. "Usually, you're the one who has to convince me to do something wild."

It was true. Of the two of them, Faith was usually more adventurous. It was a side effect of having grown up sheltered. Nowadays, she liked to take full advantage of her freedom.

"I'm not a prude," Faith said. "I just don't get all that stuff."

"Come on. There'll be cocktails. Music. Maybe even dancing."

Faith drew her fingers through her hair with a sigh.

Hadn't she just been thinking it would be fun to do something more exciting than dinner? "All right. I'll come."

"Great! I can't wait. Camilla will be happy to see you too." Lindsey told Faith the address and a time to meet. "Text me when you get there and I'll come out and get you. The club is members only, but I'll put you on the list as my guest."

"Okay. So, what exactly do I wear to a place like that?"

"You don't have to wear leather and chains if that's what you're wondering," Lindsey said. "Just dress like you're going to a high-end club. And if you want to look the part, wear something black."

CHAPTER FOUR

I'm out front.
　　Faith pressed send and waited for Lindsey in front of the club. From the outside, it was little more than a black door with a sign hanging above it that read 'Lilith's Den'. The secrecy of it all was exciting. Lindsey had mentioned that the club was exclusive, catering only to the uber-rich. What was it like inside?

A minute later, Lindsey emerged. Her auburn hair was loose, and she wore an expensive-looking black dress and heels, both of which her outrageously wealthy girlfriend had probably gifted her. Around her neck was an elaborate leather choker. Faith was sure that had been gifted to Lindsey by her girlfriend too. And she was pretty sure it wasn't just a choker.

"It's so good to see you." Lindsey pulled Faith into a hug. "Sorry again for the mix-up."

"It's okay," Faith said. "Honestly, I could use a night out. And a few drinks."

"The new job not going well, then?"

"It's just... taxing." That was one way to describe how working for Eve made Faith feel.

"Let's go in," Lindsey said.

Faith followed her through the black door into a small foyer. A large woman guarded the inner door, and another sat behind a desk beside it holding a tablet.

The woman addressed Lindsey. "A guest of yours?"

"Yep. She should be on the list. Faith Campbell."

The woman scanned her tablet and handed Faith a clipboard. "Sign these."

Faith flicked through the papers on the clipboard. There were several pages, all filled with threatening legalese. What kind of place was this that she needed to sign her life away just to step through the door?

Lindsey sensed Faith's hesitation. "Don't worry, it's just club rules, some waivers. An NDA. The people who go here just like to know their privacy is protected, for obvious reasons." She lowered her voice. "Don't be surprised if you see a famous face or two inside. Just remember, what happens at Lilith's stays at Lilith's."

Faith signed the papers and handed the clipboard back to the woman. The bouncer opened the inner door for them and nodded to Faith. "Welcome to Lilith's Den."

Faith walked through the door, staring around in awe. The dark club was packed with women, all of them drinking, chatting, and dancing. Most were dressed in all black, some in cocktail dresses and suits, others in leather, corsets, and sky-high stilettos. A few had collars and restraints on, wearing them as casually as jewelry.

The club itself was so lavish. It was like she'd entered another world, one of luxury beyond imagining. The people, the drinks, the decor—it all spoke of opulence and grandeur with a dash of sin.

A couple walked by, one in a latex bodysuit, the other wearing nothing but a thong and a thick leather collar with metal spikes. Faith gaped at her. All this kink and debauchery? It didn't bother Faith. It was kind of thrilling.

Clearly, she'd been spending too much time with Lindsey.

"We're over there." Lindsey pointed to a dimly lit corner where her girlfriend sat with another dark-haired woman Faith didn't know.

They headed over to the table. As soon as Camilla spotted them, she stood up and embraced Faith warmly.

"Lovely to see you," Camilla kissed the air next to Faith's cheek. "Has Lindsey told you about our party coming up?"

"Yep. I'll be there." Faith never turned down an invitation to go to Lindsey and Camilla's mansion, especially when there was a party involved.

Lindsey introduced Faith to the woman sitting next to Camilla. "This is Vanessa. She owns Lilith's Den."

"Nice to meet you." Vanessa folded her arms on the table in front of her. "I hear it's your first time here?"

"Yes," Faith said.

"And what do you think of my little club?"

"It's... interesting."

A smile played on Vanessa's lips. "Don't worry, no one in here bites. Not unless you want them to."

Faith's skin flushed. She sat down next to Lindsey. A few minutes later, they were joined by Vanessa's fiancée, along with a couple of other women. Lindsey introduced them to Faith, but she was so overwhelmed by everything around her that she forgot their names. Somehow, she ended up with a cocktail in her hand.

It wasn't long before the conversation turned to people and things Faith knew nothing about. Her eyes drifted around the room. In one corner, a tall, curvy woman stood beside a cage, inside which another woman knelt. Nearby, a woman was tied to a cross, another woman pressed against her, her hand up the inside of the bound woman's top. The woman on the cross had a look of ecstasy on her face.

Suddenly, the room felt warm.

"See, I told you this was boring," Lindsey said.

Faith tore her eyes away. "Hm?"

"Oh?" Lindsey grinned. "I thought that distant look in your eyes was because you were bored, not because you were distracted. Something catch your interest?"

Faith crossed her arms. "No."

"It's nothing to be embarrassed about."

"I'm not embarrassed, because I'm not interested in any of this." She gestured across the room. "I don't want to be stuffed in a cage!"

Lindsey rolled her eyes. "Do you think Camilla stuffs *me* in a cage? Although that might just be because she hasn't thought of that yet." She glanced at her girlfriend. "Anyway, all this stuff, it isn't about whips and cages. It isn't even about sex, or anything physical. It's about so much more than that."

"I know." Faith and Lindsey had had this conversation a dozen times before. But it wasn't the sexual side of this kinky world that Faith was disturbed by. Although she'd been brought up to see desire of any kind as shameful, she'd gotten over it long ago. These days, she was pretty adventurous when it came to her sexuality.

No, Faith knew all too well what these kinds of relationships were about. Submission. Power. Control. And Faith hated being controlled. She hated being powerless.

A waitress wandered past. Faith caught her eye and ordered another drink, then changed the subject. She and Lindsey had plenty to catch up on.

But as the night wore on, Faith's eyes kept wandering around the club. At the far end, there was a small stage on which a near-naked woman was suspended from the ceiling, being tied up in all kinds of knots by another woman, all in front of the watching audience. Lindsey and the others were paying it all no mind, but Faith couldn't help but stare. It was so sensual. So erotic.

Something stirred inside her. What would that feel like? To be tied up and helpless, at the mercy of another woman? She examined the bound woman's face. It was so euphoric. What was it about all this that could make someone feel that way?

Beside her, Lindsey finished off her drink. Her eyes flicked to the dance floor. "Want to go dance?"

"Sure," Faith replied. The fact that there was a dance floor was just about the only normal thing about this club. And right now, Faith needed a dose of normal.

Lindsey leaned over to where Camilla sat nearby and spoke quietly to her. Camilla nodded, then kissed her passionately, as if she were leaving for another country rather than just the dance floor.

Faith rolled her eyes. Although she was happy that her friend had found love, Lindsey and Camilla had been together for a year now, and they still hadn't left that honeymoon period. It was sickeningly sweet. Faith couldn't help but envy them. Sometimes, she wondered if that kind of love would ever exist for her. After all, life had taught her that love always came with strings.

Lindsey pried herself away from Camilla and pulled Faith to the dance floor. They'd had a few drinks, and Faith was feeling the buzz. She let herself get carried away by the music and the crowd, the glamour and the flickering lights. It didn't take long before she was lost in this dark, twisted world.

Faith's eyes flicked over to the cage in the corner again. The woman inside hadn't left it all night. The other woman sat perched on top of the cage now.

Suddenly, the woman atop the cage met Faith's eye across the room and shot Faith a smile that reminded her of a large cat.

Faith looked away sharply, wiping her brow. She and Lindsey had been dancing for some time now, and she was starting to sweat. She leaned toward Lindsey and yelled over the music. "I'm going to grab a drink."

Lindsey nodded. Faith headed to the bar and asked for a glass of water. She'd had too many cocktails already. As she gulped her glass of water down, someone sidled up beside her.

"Hey."

Faith turned. Next to her stood the woman who had been sitting on the top of the cage. Now, standing before Faith in impractically high heels, she seemed positively Amazonian.

"First time here?" the woman asked.

Faith frowned. "What gave it away?"

"You just have that look." The woman smiled. "Like a kid in a candy store." She leaned down against the bar in a way that highlighted her generous chest. "I saw you dancing out there. You look like a woman who isn't afraid to take a walk on the wild side. Want someone to show you what this place is about?"

"Uh…" Faith had to admit, she was intrigued by everything around her. But she wasn't interested in this stranger.

She glanced toward the cage where the other woman waited.

"Don't worry about her," the woman said. "My girlfriend likes having another submissive to play with."

"What makes you think I'm a submissive?"

The woman raised an eyebrow. "So you prefer the other end of the whip?"

"No. I don't." Faith held up her hands. "I appreciate the offer, but I'm not interested. All this, it isn't for me."

"If you say so." The woman straightened up. "Come find me if you change your mind and I'll give you a taste. Of course, I might make you grovel first." The woman winked at her before walking away.

Faith shook herself and finished off her glass of water. She'd wanted an interesting night out, and she'd certainly gotten that. As she turned back toward the dance floor, something caught her eye. No, not something.

Someone.

Standing by the bar, half shrouded in darkness, was a woman. Her blonde hair was dead straight, the sharp ends of it grazing her bare shoulders. She was dressed in a black corset of silk and lace that cinched her waist tight, along with a short leather skirt, fishnet stockings, and heels.

Faith stared, unable to tear her eyes away. The woman gave off this unmistakable air of superiority that immediately told Faith that she was a Domme. The room was full of women like her, but this woman was different. She radiated this confidence that was so captivating.

But that wasn't all that drew Faith's eye. The woman?

She almost looked like Eve.

It was a crazy thought. Faith couldn't even see the woman's face. Was this mixed up attraction Faith felt toward Eve so bad that her mind was seeing Eve everywhere?

Suddenly, the woman turned Faith's way. Their eyes locked.

Faith's heart stopped. *It can't be.* The woman looked so much like Eve. Her face was expressionless, but she had a dark, overpowering look in her eyes that set something deep inside Faith's body alight—

"Faith?"

She felt a hand on her arm. She spun around. Lindsey stood beside her.

"I saw that woman hitting on you. Thought you might need rescuing." She looked at Faith's face, her brows drawing together. "Everything okay?"

"Yeah. I'm fine." Faith glanced over her shoulder.

The woman in the corset was gone.

"Are you sure?" Lindsey asked.

"It's nothing. I thought I saw someone, that's all." Faith shook her head. She needed to sit down. "Come on. Let's go back to the others."

As they returned to the table, she looked back toward where the woman in the corset had been standing. There was no sign of her. Either she'd disappeared into the crowd, or she'd been no more than an apparition in the first place. Either way, one thing was certain.

The woman hadn't been Eve.

CHAPTER FIVE

A few days passed before Faith returned to work for Eve. And in those few days, Faith had thought about nothing but the woman in the corset from Lilith's Den. In her mind's eye, she couldn't stop seeing Eve's face on her.

It was almost like Faith was hoping the woman *was* Eve. But that didn't make any sense. Faith wasn't interested in Eve. She wasn't interested in that world of submission and power games that the woman in the corset was so clearly a part of either. So why was she obsessing about both of them?

And why did thinking about them make her hot all over?

Faith let herself into the house. She had a few minutes before she had to wake the twins up and get them ready for school. As she walked down the hall, she spotted Eve in the kitchen. Her hair was styled in her usual short curled bob, and she was dressed for work.

Eve turned and spotted her. "Good morning, Faith."

Faith entered the kitchen. "Hi."

Eve continued making her breakfast. Faith watched her as she did. Surely if she'd been at Lilith's Den that night she'd show Faith some kind of sign. It wasn't impossible that the woman had been Eve. If Eve swapped out her glasses for contact lenses and straightened her hair, she'd look just like her. And Eve hadn't had the twins that night. Would she have spent one of her rare free nights at Lilith's Den? And on a 'ladies only' night? Faith had no idea if Eve was interested in women. She'd been married to a man, but that didn't mean anything. Faith herself wasn't fussy about the gender of who she dated. Sexuality, attraction, love—it had never been one or the other to her. Perhaps Eve felt the same way.

Eve held up the pot of coffee. "Would you like some? I just made it."

"Sure," Faith replied.

Eve got out two mugs and filled them both with coffee. She handed one to Faith. Their fingers brushed. Faith nearly dropped the cup.

She muttered a thank you and took a sip, peering at Eve as she did so. Did Eve have a sister? An identical twin? One who was the opposite of her in every way? Well, not every way. Eve had the same domineering air. But while Eve was more likely to scold Faith for putting the milk in the wrong part of the fridge, she suspected the woman in the corset was a completely different kind of controlling.

Could they be one and the same? Could it be that behind this mother and businesswoman was a passionate Domme dying to come out?

Could Faith be the one to bring her out?

Why did she want that? She'd never had such desires

before, not until that night at Lilith's Den. And seeing Eve, here and now, only made them stronger. She peered at Eve again. The resemblance was uncanny. What if they were the same person?

And if that were the case, which was the real Eve?

"Is something the matter?" Eve asked.

Faith shook her head. "No. It's fine."

The toaster popped. Eve plucked out her toast and began buttering it.

Faith steadied herself. It was time for her to start the morning routine. But something held her there in the kitchen.

She had to know.

She cleared her throat. "So, did you get up to anything while the twins were away?"

"What do you mean?" Eve asked.

"You know, did you do anything? Go anywhere?"

"I didn't do anything unusual." Eve narrowed her eyes. "Why?"

"No reason," Faith said quickly. "I'm just curious. I don't know much about you. Like, what you do in your spare time. For fun."

"I work full time, and until now I've been raising two kids by myself. It doesn't leave me with a lot of time for fun."

"Right." This was silly. Faith picked up her mug and headed out of the kitchen.

"What about you?"

"Huh?" Faith turned in the doorway to see Eve looking at her, her plate in one hand and coffee in another. Her eyes were dark behind her glasses.

"Did you do anything *fun* during your time off?"

"I... Yes." There was something suggestive in Eve's voice. Or was Faith imagining it?

Eve took a few steps toward her, cornering her by the doorway. Faith could feel the heat of her body. "And what did you get up to?"

Faith hesitated. "I went to a club. With a friend. On Tuesday." She didn't dare be any more specific. The way Eve was looking at her made Faith feel exposed.

"Did you enjoy yourself?" Eve asked.

Faith's voice caught in her throat. "Yes. I did."

Eve stepped closer. Faith froze. Her heart was beating so hard, she was sure Eve could hear it. Was Faith right after all? Had Eve been at Lilith's Den that night, dressed in a corset?

Did Eve know all about the sinful thoughts going through Faith's mind?

"Good," Eve said. "With me working you so hard, you should be making the most of your days off." She slipped past Faith, through the doorway and out into the hall. "I'll be in the dining room if you need me."

Faith let out a breath. As she watched Eve walk away, hips swaying in her fitted skirt, she couldn't help but notice how much Eve's figure was like that of the woman in the corset.

Faith looked at her watch. It was time to pick up the twins from school. She grabbed her things and left her apartment. After finishing with the chores and errands Eve had given her in the morning, she'd gone home to have a lunch break. It was with Eve's permission, of course. She didn't do anything without Eve's permission.

She'd never had a job where she'd had to deal with this level of supervision, but she was getting used to it. The fact that she was being paid double her usual rate certainly helped. Plus, the twins were easy kids. As far as jobs went, this was a good one.

All Faith had to do was quash the inexplicable attraction she felt toward Eve, along with her obsession with Eve being the woman in the corset from Lilith's Den.

Faith headed down to her car. As she passed the mailboxes for the apartment, she noticed a letter sticking out of hers. Her heart leaped. Only one person ever wrote to Faith—her sister, Abigail. She and Faith had an arrangement. Abigail would write to her one month, and Faith would send her a letter in reply the next month. They'd been doing so for years, every month like clockwork. It was the only way they could communicate without the rest of their family catching on. But it had been more than two months since Faith had last heard from Abigail. She'd been waiting for a letter for weeks now.

She rushed over to her mailbox and yanked the letter out.

Her heart sank. It was a phone bill.

Faith stuffed the letter back into her mailbox, pushing her disappointment aside. She had to go pick up the twins. But as she sat in the car and drove to the twins' school, her mind wandered back to her sister. Why hadn't she written? There were so many possibilities, all of them awful. Was she sick? Injured? Did something terrible happen to her? Or worse—had someone else from her family found out that Abigail had been writing to Faith in secret? That would be bad news for her sister.

There was no point in speculating. Abigail was probably just busy. After all, she was married with a family of her own now, despite being even younger than Faith. That was perfectly normal in the community her family lived in.

Faith reached the elite private school the twins attended and went through the usual pickup procedure. It was routine now. As Eve had helpfully reminded her in the morning, Ethan had soccer practice in the afternoon, and Leah had a violin lesson.

Faith dropped Ethan off first. As she drove Leah to her violin tutor's house, she glanced at Leah in the rearview mirror. Leah hadn't said much the whole drive. She was a quiet kid, quieter than her brother, but this was unusual even for her.

"Leah?" Faith asked. "Is something the matter?"

Leah pouted. "We had a spelling test today. Ethan beat me."

"Well, how did you do in the test?"

"I got two words wrong."

"So you got all the rest right?" Faith asked. "You did amazingly. Just because Ethan did better doesn't mean you didn't do great too." Both the twins were practically geniuses, which wasn't surprising considering how hard their mother pushed them.

"But he's going to tell Mom, and Mom is going to be upset at me," Leah said.

"She's not going to be upset. I'm sure she'll be very proud of you."

Leah sighed. "She's never happy when I don't do as good as Ethan."

Faith frowned. Now that Leah mentioned it, Eve did seem a little more critical of Leah than she was of Ethan. It was just one of the many things about Eve that Faith didn't understand.

As they pulled out the front of Leah's tutor's house, Faith's phone buzzed on the seat next to her. She parked the car and grabbed the phone. She had a message from Eve.

Leah's tutor called to cancel. Take her home instead.

Faith sent Eve a reply and turned to Leah in the back seat. "No violin lesson for you today. Your tutor canceled."

"Oh." Leah's shoulders slumped. Playing the violin was one of the few activities Eve made Leah do that she actually seemed to enjoy.

"You can practice at home instead," Faith said. "I'll help. Or better yet, you can put on a concert for me. I'd love to hear you play."

"I guess," Leah mumbled. She looked out the window toward a park just down the road. Her eyes lit up. "Can we go to the park instead?"

Faith shook her head. "Not today. It's time to go home."

"Please? Just for a little bit?"

Faith sighed. Leah looked like she could use some cheering up. "Okay," she said. "Just ten minutes. Then we're going home."

Faith unlocked the front door and ushered Leah inside.

"Let's go make a snack. Then you can put on that concert for me."

"Okay." Leah grinned and bounced down the hall.

Faith followed her into the kitchen. She opened the fridge. All the ingredients for Eve's pre-approved healthy snacks were right there on the shelves. Perhaps Faith could mix things up a bit, make something a little more interesting-

"Mom!" Leah said. "You're here!"

Faith turned. Eve was standing in the doorway, her eyes dark and her arms crossed.

She did not look happy.

"Eve," Faith said. "You're home."

"I finished up at work early." Eve looked down at Leah. "Why don't you go upstairs, sweetie? I need to talk to Faith."

"Okay." Leah skipped out of the kitchen, oblivious to the displeasure radiating from her mother.

"Faith," Eve said. "Come with me." She turned on her heel and started down the hall.

Faith followed Eve toward the back of the house and into her office. What did Eve want? Her voice had taken on the exact same tone she used when one of the twins was in trouble.

Eve shut the door and gestured to a chair in the middle of the room. "Have a seat."

Faith sat down.

Eve stood before her, looming over Faith's chair. "You were supposed to be home twenty minutes ago."

That was what this was about? "We were at the park," Faith said.

"Did I say you could take Leah to the park?"

"No. But it was just down the road from her tutor's house. We were already there when I got your message."

"And how was I supposed to know where you were?" Eve said coldly. "Where Leah was?"

"I'm sorry," Faith said. "I thought you were at wor—"

"That makes it okay for you to take Leah somewhere without my permission?"

"It was just for a little while. I didn't think you'd mind."

"I *do* mind. I've set out a schedule for them which I expect you to follow." Her face darkened. "Is this something you've been doing? Taking the twins places I haven't approved?"

"No, of course not," Faith said. "This was a one-off. I'll ask first next time."

"There won't be a next time." Eve put her hands on her hips. "You're not taking Leah or Ethan anywhere other than where I tell you to. You're not to do anything with them unless I've given you explicit permission. You're not to deviate from the instructions I've given you in any way."

Faith bit back her frustration. How was she supposed to do her job if she couldn't do anything without Eve's approval?

"Well?" Eve said. "Do you have something to say?"

"It's just—" Faith chose her words carefully. "I know I'm not their mother, but when the twins are with me it's my job to look after them. And it's hard to do that if I can't make judgment calls sometimes. Leah was upset. I was trying to cheer her up. I thought going to the park would help. It was only for twenty minutes. I brought her straight home after that."

Eve frowned. "Leah was upset? What about?"

"Just a test at school." Faith didn't elaborate. Telling Eve that Leah was upset because she didn't want Eve to be disappointed in her wouldn't go down well at the best of times.

"That's no excuse," Eve snapped. "I'm her mother, not you. I decide where she goes and what she does." She leaned down over Faith's chair. "You will do as I say, or I'll find another nanny who can follow my instructions."

"Okay." Faith spoke through gritted teeth. "I won't do it again." She didn't apologize. She'd just been doing her job, but Eve was behaving as though Faith had taken Leah to some seedy back alley, not the park.

Eve scowled. "Just go home. I can handle the kids for the rest of the night." She walked over to the door and opened it wide.

Faith left the room in a huff. She'd thought this job had been going well, but Eve was more infuriating than anyone else she'd worked for. And to think, just hours before, Faith had been having all kinds of crazy thoughts about her. It was ridiculous. Eve was Eve, not this mysterious woman in a corset that Faith had been obsessing about.

And Faith wasn't interested in either of them.

CHAPTER SIX

Faith arrived at the front of Lindsey and Camilla's house. It was evening and the grounds of the estate looked stunning in the fading light. She loved coming out here, to this little slice of paradise just outside the city. The huge estate was like its own little world.

She got out of the car and looked up at the mansion before her. She'd been here a dozen times now, but she still found it impressive. It made Eve's suburban palace look tiny in comparison.

Stop thinking about Eve. Faith had the whole weekend off. She was at her best friend's party. She was supposed to be letting her hair down.

So why couldn't she get Eve out of her mind?

The tension between the two of them had only risen since that afternoon in Eve's office. It was like Eve had been watching Faith's every move, her eyes dark and inscrutable behind her glasses. And every time Eve was around, it made

Faith simmer inside with something that wasn't entirely annoyance.

A weekend away from Eve was exactly what she needed. Hopefully, it would help clear her head.

Faith headed into the house. Inside the entrance hall, Faith paused by a mirror to straighten out her outfit. The dress she wore, a knee-length blue number, had been borrowed from Lindsey. She didn't own many dresses that were fancy enough for an occasion like this. These parties Lindsey's girlfriend threw weren't Faith's usual scene, but she still loved attending them. They were so glamourous.

She fixed her hair, which she'd managed to style into loose waves instead of her usual messy curls, and followed a pair of guests to the ballroom. The party was in full swing, the room filled with dozens of people. She scanned the crowd until she found Lindsey. She was standing with her girlfriend by a table of canapés.

As Faith approached her friend, Lindsey spotted her. She rushed over to Faith and pulled her to the side, a sheepish look on her face.

"What's going on?" Faith asked.

"It's Eve," Lindsey said. "She's here."

Faith's stomach flipped. "What's she doing here?"

"Camilla invited her. I didn't realize she was *your* Eve until Camilla introduced us. We were all talking, and she mentioned some stuff that sounded familiar, like her job and that she had twins, and it clicked."

Great. That was just Faith's luck. She'd left the city, and she still couldn't escape Eve. "Where is she?"

Lindsey pointed to the other side of the room. Amid a group of people stood a stunning blonde woman holding a glass of champagne. Her back was turned, her hair straight and parted to one side. She wore a strapless black gown that went down to the floor. Faith wouldn't have been able to tell that the woman was Eve if she hadn't recognized the dress. She had seen it in Eve's closet, tucked away with all her other glamourous clothes.

Dressed like this, Eve looked even more like the woman in the corset.

"How does Camilla know her?" Faith asked.

Lindsey shrugged. "I haven't had a chance to ask. Camilla has never mentioned her before. I think they're just part of the same rich people social circle."

Faith glanced at Eve. "So they don't know each other from Lilith's Den?"

"Not that I know of. Why?"

"No reason," Faith said quickly.

"I hope this doesn't make things awkward," Lindsey said. "I know she's been giving you a hard time at work."

"It's fine." Faith had told Lindsey about how Eve had dressed her down in her office that afternoon. But that was only part of the reason Faith was frustrated with Eve.

Faith pulled herself together. She was not going to let Eve's presence ruin a good party. "So, where are the drinks?"

Lindsey led her over to the bar where Faith grabbed a glass of champagne. It was crisp and light, more delicious than any champagne Faith had ever tasted. She and Lindsey sat down in a quiet corner to talk. It wasn't long before Camilla found them and dragged them both off to meet people.

The evening wore on, the sky darkening to night outside

the wide windows of the ballroom. After finishing off her second glass of champagne, Faith excused herself and went back to the bar for another drink. This time, she asked for a glass of rosé. It had just the right balance of sweetness.

She sighed contentedly. She was enjoying herself. Although she had little in common with most of the people in the room, there was delicious food, top-shelf drinks, and interesting conversation. It was enough to make her forget about Eve.

Almost.

Faith searched the room for her. Did Eve know she was here? The party was so big that Faith hadn't crossed paths with her yet.

Her eyes landed on Eve. She was nearby, deep in conversation with a pair of women, close enough that Faith could see her face. Without her glasses, the long, dark lashes that framed Eve's hazel eyes made their depths seem endless. Her cheeks had a faint flush, and her lips were a pale shade of pink that brought to mind the rosé Faith was drinking.

Would Eve's lips taste just as sweet?

As if overhearing Faith's thoughts, Eve turned toward her. There was a flash of surprise in Eve's eyes, followed by something else. A cool fire that made Faith burn inside. It was just like that night at Lilith's Den, that moment Faith had locked eyes with the woman in the corset.

Faith turned around sharply and took a deep breath. A minute passed, then two, then five, but Eve didn't approach her. And Faith didn't dare look for her again.

Faith finished off her glass of rosé and went off to mingle again. She didn't know why she was avoiding Eve. She had no reason to hide from her. But Eve hadn't sought her out either. Was she avoiding Faith too? Faith wasn't sure whether to be relieved or offended. She had no idea what she wanted from Eve.

She shook her head. She was being ridiculous. She couldn't avoid Eve all night. It was better to just speak to her, to get it out of the way.

And there was no time like the present.

She scanned the room for Eve again. This time, Faith found her sitting alone, her head down and her hair falling over her face, half hiding it from view. Faith steeled herself and headed over to her.

As Faith approached her, Eve didn't look up. Her eyes were fixed on the phone in her hand, a worried look on her face. Before Faith could reach her, Eve stood up and stormed out of the room.

Faith frowned. Was Eve upset? It took a lot to upset Eve. Faith hesitated, then followed her out the door.

The hall beyond led deeper into the mansion. Eve was already out of sight, but Faith could hear her voice faintly. As Faith followed her down the hall, the sounds of the party receded behind her, and Eve's voice grew louder. Eve was almost yelling, but Faith couldn't make out the words. Eve's voice became more agitated, then stopped abruptly.

Faith reached an open doorway and peered into the room beyond. It was a library of some kind, with books covering every inch of the walls. In the corner, Eve sat perched on the arm of an armchair, scowling at her phone.

Faith knocked on the door.

Eve looked up. "Faith."

"I saw you leave. You looked worried." Faith slipped into the room. "I just wanted to make sure everything's okay."

"You're not on the clock. You don't need to worry about me."

"I know I don't have to, but I do."

Eve let out a hard sigh. "I've been calling Harrison all evening so I could say goodnight to the twins, but he wouldn't pick up his phone. When I finally got through, his mother answered and said the twins were already asleep." Her grip on the phone tightened. "Of course they're asleep now. If someone had answered the phone an hour ago, I would have been able to talk to them before they went to bed." She shook her head. "I'm sure they're fine. I'm just sick to death of Eleanor's petty tricks. I have no doubt this was deliberate. She's been pulling this kind of thing for years."

Faith gave her a sympathetic look. "She sounds like a real piece of work."

"You don't know the half of it. I just wanted one night off, to not have to worry about the twins and all this custody business, yet here I am." Eve placed her phone down on the desk next to her. "What are you doing here, anyway?"

"I'm friends with Lindsey. We went to art school together. What about you?"

"Camilla invited me."

Faith hesitated. "How do you know each other?"

"I don't remember exactly. We have a mutual friend or two, so we run into each other a lot, but we don't know each other well."

Silence fell over them. Faith walked over to the window and looked out it. She had no reason to stay in this room anymore. But something held her there. Eve held her there.

Eve got up from the armchair and joined Faith by the window. "It's a lovely view, isn't it?"

Faith nodded. Outside, the moonlit estate grounds stretched on and on. Faith kept her eyes fixed on the view, not daring to look at Eve. Being alone with her, standing so close to her, set off the exact same feeling in Faith that the woman in the corset had.

"Look," Eve said. "About the other day, in my office. I'm sorry for the way I treated you. I shouldn't have yelled at you."

"It's okay," Faith replied. "You were just looking out for Leah's best interests."

"No, it wasn't about Leah. It was about me." Eve's eyes grew distant. "This is the first time I've ever let anyone else be responsible for my kids. I've been feeling so conflicted about it. I took it out on you."

"It's fine," Faith said. "Really, I understand."

"I know I can be controlling and critical, but you should know, I'm very happy about the job you're doing. I'd be lost without you. So thank you."

"No problem," Faith said. "I'm just doing my job."

"No, you're doing far more than that. You seem to really care about the twins. You have a way with them."

"They're great kids. Working with the twins is effortless. I enjoy it."

Eve turned to look at her. "And how do you find working with their mother?"

Faith smiled. "It's not bad either."

"Well, I appreciate everything you do for us." Eve touched Faith's arm. "And I appreciate having you around."

Faith's skin prickled. Suddenly, all those feelings of frustration Faith harbored for Eve were replaced with something else entirely.

"Is something the matter?" Eve asked.

"No," Faith replied. "It's just, you seem so different. You look different. The hair, the glasses, the dress. You look stunning."

Eve swept her eyes down Faith's body. "You don't look too bad yourself."

Suddenly, Faith felt very naked. "The dress isn't mine. I borrowed it from Lindsey."

"It looks like it was made for you." Eve took a step closer. "You seem different too, you know. You're much more relaxed outside work. More free. Wilder."

Faith's heart thumped hard against her chest. "Outside work?" Could she mean at Lilith's Den?

Eve didn't respond.

Faith drew in a breath. She couldn't stay silent any longer. She had to know the answer to the question etched on her mind or she'd never know peace again.

"Eve," she said. "Was it you?"

Eve tilted her head to the side, studying Faith. "Was what me?"

"Was it you, the other night at Lilith's Den? In the corset?" Faith searched Eve's eyes. They gave nothing away. Was she wrong? Had she imagined it all? "I have to know. Was it you?"

Eve didn't answer her at first. She just stared back at Faith, holding her in place with her gaze.

Finally, Eve spoke.

"Yes. It was me."

CHAPTER SEVEN

Faith stood frozen on the spot. She knew it. Eve and the woman in the corset were one and the same. "I haven't been able to stop thinking about her," she blurted out. "About you. About how much I wanted you to be her—"

Eve pressed her finger to Faith's lips. "Wait."

Faith nodded. Eve removed her finger. Faith's lips tingled.

Eve walked over to the door, shut it, and returned to Faith's side. "Tell me again. What were you saying?"

Faith spoke softly. "Ever since that night, I haven't been able to stop thinking about you." She looked into Eve's eyes. "I want you so badly, Eve."

Eve brought her hand up, her eyes smoldering, and drew it down Faith's cheek. "From the moment I laid eyes on you at Lilith's Den, all I've wanted to do was make you mine."

A tremor went through Faith's body. In the space of a heartbeat, Eve's lips were on Faith's, kissing her so furiously that she had to grab onto Eve's shoulder to steady herself.

Eve's fingers curled in Faith's hair, her other hand around Faith's waist, pulling her close.

She closed her eyes, letting Eve's lips and arms engulf her. Eve's hunger and intensity took Faith back to that night at Lilith's Den the moment their eyes had met. This was the woman in the corset, the one who had made Faith breathless with just a glance. This was the woman who had filled her daydreams with all kinds of wicked images.

This was the woman who had made her realize she wanted something she never, ever thought she'd want.

Faith swept her hand up the side of Eve's neck, her other hand tightening around Eve's waist. Eve's body pressed against hers, pushing her back into the window. Faith trembled. The glass was cold against her bare shoulders, but the rest of her was on fire.

Eve slid her palm down Faith's chest, grazing it over her breast. Faith's nipples tightened under her dress. She slid her hand down the swell of Eve's hip, feeling the fullness of her curves. Eve grabbed hold of Faith's ass cheek, drawing her impossibly closer. A desperate murmur fell from Faith's lips.

Eve ran a hand down Faith's thigh, her fingertips seeking out the hem of Faith's dress. She dragged it up Faith's leg. Faith's pulse sped up. Was this really happening? Were they really doing this, here and now, just a few rooms away from a party full of people?

Eve broke away. Conflict and desire swirled behind her eyes, mixing with the greens and browns of her irises. "You want this?" It was as much a statement as it was a question.

"Yes," Faith said. "More than anything."

Eve kissed her again, hot and hard. Her lips still locked

on Faith's, she slipped her hand between Faith's thighs. Faith's grip on Eve's hip tightened, heat flaring within her. She pushed back against Eve, spurring her on.

Breaking the kiss, Eve pulled Faith's dress all the way up to her waist and hooked her fingers into the sides of Faith's panties, pushing them down past her hips. They fell to the floor. Faith's whole body pulsed with need.

With painstaking slowness, Eve drew her hand up the inside of Faith's leg, all the way to the peak of her thighs. She slipped her fingers between Faith's swollen lips, sending a dart of pleasure through her.

Eve withdrew her hand and brought it up before her eyes. Her fingers were wet with Faith's arousal. "You really do want me." She drew her fingers down the center of Faith's chest, leaving a trail of her wetness down between Faith's breasts.

"Yes, I want you." After denying it for so long, Faith couldn't stop the words from spilling from her. "God, I want you."

Eve slid her hand down again. Faith's breath hitched, her head tipping back against the window. Eve ran her finger up and down Faith's slit, painting long slow strokes with her fingertips. Faith's hands scrabbled at the glass behind her. Eve's finger found Faith's hidden nub, strumming it gently.

Faith quivered. Here they were, in a darkened room at a party, with barely a few kisses for foreplay, yet Faith was already throbbing. She'd been craving Eve's touch for so long now. The hurried, forbidden nature of their tryst only made Faith hotter.

"Yes," she said. "Don't stop."

Eve pulled away, letting Faith's dress fall back down.

"After all this time, you still haven't figured me out." Eve's voice was a whispered growl. "I like to take control. I like to do things my way. And I don't take orders.""

Eve took Faith's shoulders and spun her around so that she was facing the window. Faith gasped.

From behind her, Eve brought her hand up to Faith's chest, massaging her breast through her dress. "Was that an order, Faith?"

Faith shook her head, too off-balance to speak. Eve's body was pressed against hers, and with the low-backed dress Faith wore, all that separated their bare skin was the fabric of Eve's dress. Faith could feel Eve's peaked nipples through it.

"I wasn't planning to stop." Eve leaned in, her breath tickling Faith's neck. "I was going to tease you until you couldn't take it any longer. And then I was going to make you come undone."

A ripple went through Faith's body. Eve wasn't even touching her, yet her words made Faith just as hot as when Eve had had her hand between her legs.

"Is that what you want?" Eve asked.

"Yes," Faith said. *"Please."*

Eve brushed a hand up to Faith's chin and tilted it to the side, pressing her lips against Faith's. "It seems we understand each other."

Once again, Eve drew up Faith's dress. She traced her hand up the back of Faith's leg, over her bare ass cheek, then back down to where her thighs met, seeking out her entrance. Faith bent at the waist, resisting the urge to push herself back toward the other woman. Eve seized hold of Faith's hip, holding her in place.

Faith closed her eyes, anticipation welling inside her. Slowly, Eve entered her, filling her completely. Faith let out a moan, her body threatening to collapse. Eve's fingers inside her felt so divine.

Eve thrust in and out, sending jolts of pleasure deep into Faith's body. Faith shuddered and moaned, delirious. Eve's stroking, curling fingers were unrelenting.

Eve quickened the pace. Faith rocked back against her, one of her breasts escaping from the top of her dress. Eve caressed it greedily. Far too late, Faith remembered they were standing by the window. Was anyone out there, wandering the grounds? She made a feeble attempt to pull the curtain next to her shut, but with Eve's fingers between her thighs and Eve's hand kneading her chest, she was so close—

Faith cried out as pleasure crashed through her. She pushed back into Eve, the other woman still surging inside her, and rode the waves of bliss rolling through her body.

Once Faith's orgasm receded, Eve whirled her back around and brought her lips to Faith's in a dizzying kiss. Her head spun, the world around her spinning with it. As her post-orgasm haze cleared, all the realizations from the past hour hit her. The woman in the corset was Eve. Faith's boss. And she'd just given Faith an earth-shattering orgasm up against the window at a party they both just happened to be at.

Eve drew back. "Here." She bent down, picked something up, and held it out to Faith.

Faith blinked at the bundle of fabric in Eve's hands. Her panties. "Um, thanks." She took them from Eve and slipped them back on.

"Is something wrong?" Eve asked.

"I just can't believe it, that's all," Faith said. "It was you all along. I've been wondering ever since that night. Why didn't you say anything?"

Eve smoothed down her barely tousled dress. "What was I supposed to say?"

"But I asked you about it. That morning, in the kitchen."

"And I told you the truth. I said I didn't get up to anything unusual."

"You mean, you do that a lot?" Faith said. "Put on a corset and go to Lilith's Den?"

"Every now and then. Not so much lately. I've been busy. It's probably why I've never seen you there before."

"I'd never been there before. I only went there that night because I wanted to catch up with Lindsey."

Eve raised an eyebrow. "You went to Lilith's just to catch up with a friend?"

"Yes. I'm not interested in that stuff."

"You could have fooled me."

"I mean, I wasn't interested," Faith said. "Not at first. But going to that club made me realize how much it all appealed to me. And then I saw you, and I realized how much I wanted you. And god, how I've wanted you."

Faith looked into Eve's eyes. Eve turned away. The playfulness in her gaze had disappeared.

"We should get back," Eve said. "Before anyone notices we're gone."

Faith's stomach sank. "Shouldn't we talk about this?"

As Eve opened her mouth to speak, the door to the library swung open. In strolled Camilla, a glass of wine in her hand.

"Hello." Camilla walked over to a bookshelf, barely paying them any attention. "Don't mind me, I just need to grab something."

"Camilla," Eve said. "We were just talking."

Camilla's eyes fell on the two of them. A smirk crossed her lips. "No need to explain yourselves to me. This is a party, after all. You're supposed to be enjoying yourself." She looked from one woman to the other. "And it looks like the two of you are having fun."

Blood raced to Faith's cheeks. Eve was a terrible liar. Or maybe it was the fact that Eve's hair was in disarray and Faith's dress was askew. She straightened it up.

"Here it is." Camilla plucked a book from the shelf. "I'll leave you two alone."

Camilla sauntered out of the room. Faith turned to Eve. Gone was the passionate woman in the corset. The Eve that Faith knew was back.

"I'm going back to the party." Without a further word, Eve strode out the door, leaving Faith alone in the room.

When Faith returned to the party, Eve was nowhere to be found.

CHAPTER EIGHT

When Faith returned to work a few days later, her heart was in her throat. She hadn't seen or spoken to Eve since she'd walked out of the library that night at Lindsey's party. She had no idea how Eve was going to react.

Faith herself didn't know how to react. That night with Eve had turned her world upside down. Everything the woman in the corset had awakened in her that night at Lilith's Den had gone from a half-formed fantasy to an insatiable craving.

She unlocked the front door and entered the house. "Hello," she called. "It's Faith."

She was met with an eerie silence. At this time of the morning, the kids were still asleep, but Eve was usually up and about, getting ready for the day. Faith wandered through the house, peeking into rooms as she passed. Eve wasn't in any of the lounge rooms, or the kitchen, or the dining room.

Giving up, Faith went upstairs to wake up the twins.

Once they were out of bed, she headed back downstairs to prepare their breakfast. At the base of the stairs, she almost ran into Eve.

"Good morning," Faith stammered.

"Faith," Eve said. "Are the twins up?"

Faith nodded.

"Good." Without another word, Eve walked off toward her bedroom.

Faith frowned. Was Eve avoiding her? Faith hadn't known what to expect from Eve, but this wasn't it. Just days ago, she'd had her hand up Faith's dress, whispering all kinds of dirty things in her ear, and now, this? Was Eve just going to pretend nothing had happened between them?

She went into the kitchen and began making the twins' breakfast. It was all routine now. Usually, Eve would be coming and going, giving Faith instructions. Not today.

A few minutes later, the twins came downstairs. Faith served them breakfast at the dining table and sat down across from them. Midway through the meal, Eve entered the room, greeting the kids and planting a kiss on each of their cheeks before sitting down to talk with them while they ate. Faith tried to catch her eye, but Eve avoided it. She barely acknowledged that Faith was even there.

Hurt welled up in Faith's chest. She couldn't believe Eve would be so cold. Faith had given in to all the feelings she'd been resisting for so long. Her longing for Eve. Her submissive desires. She'd exposed her deepest, darkest self to Eve.

And now, Eve was ignoring her.

Faith pushed her feelings aside. Getting upset at work was never a good idea. Then again, neither was hooking up with her boss at a party.

Once the twins finished their breakfast, Faith sent them upstairs to brush their teeth. Eve stood up to follow them out of the room.

"Eve," Faith said. "Do you have a minute?"

"I need to get ready for work." Before Faith could stop her, Eve slipped out the door.

Faith scowled. She wasn't upset anymore. She was mad. She wasn't going to let Eve brush her off. Eve wasn't going to make this easy, but Faith wasn't going to give up.

She helped the twins get ready for school. Today, they were carpooling with a friend who lived down the road, so Faith had to do little more than see them off at the street. Once they'd been picked up, she returned to the house. She had errands to run for the family. Grocery shopping, picking up school supplies. But they would have to wait.

Faith sat down at the bottom of the stairs. She didn't dare go barging into Eve's room. But sooner or later, Eve would have to walk past.

After a few minutes, Faith heard the distinctive click of heels on the marble floor. As Eve's footsteps grew closer, Faith stood up from her hiding place behind the banister, coming face-to-face with Eve.

Eve startled, almost dropping her briefcase. "Faith." She looked at her watch. "I need to get going."

"No." Faith crossed her arms. "You've been avoiding me all morning."

"I don't have time for this."

"I don't care." The intensity in Faith's voice surprised even Faith herself. "Why are you ignoring me?"

"I'm not ignoring you."

"Yes, you are."

"Fine," Eve said. "I am."

"Why?"

"Isn't it obvious?"

Faith flinched. "Do you regret what happened between us?"

"Believe me," Eve said. "That's not it."

"Then what is it?" This was like pulling teeth. "You won't talk to me, you'll barely look at me. You won't even be alone in a room with me! If you don't regret it, then why are you acting like this?"

Eve stiffened. Faith could see the battle going on in her mind. Still, Eve didn't speak.

"Eve, please! Just talk to me."

"You want to know why I've been avoiding you?" Eve said softly.

"Yes!"

Eve took a few steps toward Faith until they were almost touching. Her eyes blazed. "I've been avoiding you because I was afraid that if I was alone with you I wouldn't be able to hold myself back."

Faith's breath caught in her chest. Right there and then Faith realized that the difference between Eve and the woman in the corset had nothing to do with Eve's hair, or her clothes, or her glasses. It was this. This intensity that radiated from every part of her, from her gaze, to her stance, to her voice. That was what the woman in the corset possessed that Eve didn't. No, it was in Eve too, hiding behind that prim, proper woman.

All Eve had to do was let that side of her out.

"Then don't," Faith said. "Don't hold back."

Tentatively, Faith brought her hand up to Eve's cheek.

Eve seized Faith's wrist in midair. Faith's heart began to race. They stood there, unmoving, searching each other's eyes. Eve's were filled with conflict and lust.

"Don't hold back," Faith whispered.

At once, Eve's lips crashed against Faith's in a firm, unyielding kiss. Faith crumbled. This was the woman from the other night, Eve and the woman in the corset all rolled into one. This was the woman who made Faith come undone.

She deepened the kiss, clutching at Eve's neck to anchor herself against the force of Eve's passion. The hard railing of the stairs pressed into her back, Eve's body pinning her to it. Her lips parted and their tongues swirled against each other. A soft purr rose from Faith's chest.

Eve jerked away. "We shouldn't."

Faith stifled a groan. "Why not?"

"You work for me. You're my nanny. And I just got divorced, and the twins… This is all so *wrong*."

"What's wrong about this?"

"It's complicated. Believe me when I say this is just a bad idea." Eve's voice dropped low. "But I don't want to stop."

Eve let go of her briefcase. It fell to the floor with a thump. She pressed her lips to Faith's again and wrapped her hands up around Faith's waist, pulling her closer. Her lips traveled down Faith's cheek. Faith tipped her head back, baring her neck. Eve's kisses turned into gentle bites. One of Eve's hands roamed up to Faith's chest, groping her breast through her blouse. Faith let out a strangled whimper, her hands grabbing at Eve's curves.

Eve pulled back again. "We can't. Not now. I meant it when I said I need to go to work."

"No," Faith protested. "Stay."

Eve shot her a stern look. "What did I tell you that night in the library?"

Faith got even hotter at the thought. "That you don't like orders."

"Exactly."

"Stay, *please*?" Faith asked sweetly.

A faint chuckle rose from Eve's chest. "I would if I could." Eve took Faith's wrists and pried them from her waist. "But I have to go. I'll see you in the evening. We'll talk then." Eve kissed her again, then picked up the briefcase. "Don't forget to pick up milk while you're at the store. And remember, the twins have a dentist appointment after school."

Faith sighed. It seemed Eve still wasn't prepared to let go of control in that area of their relationship either.

CHAPTER NINE

So, when were you going to tell me about you and Eve?

Faith cursed to herself. The message was from Lindsey. She should have known that Camilla wouldn't have been able to keep something like that from her girlfriend.

It just kind of happened, Faith typed out. No, that was a lie. Everything between her and Eve had been brewing for so long. It had only been a matter of time before it boiled over. And now Faith's whole world had been turned upside down.

Faith placed her phone down on the coffee table without sending a reply and sat back to wait for Eve. It was 8 p.m., but Eve had been held up at the office.

The sound of the front door opening reached Faith's ears, followed by Eve's footsteps. A moment later, Eve entered the lounge room. She possessed her usual poise, but her face showed a hint of weariness. However, there was a spark of the woman Faith had glimpsed in the morning there.

"Thanks for taking care of everything for me," Eve said.

"No problem," Faith replied. "I just put the twins to bed if you want to say goodnight to them. Leah could use it."

"Is she all right?"

"She was upset all afternoon. She didn't want to do her homework. She's been struggling a little with it lately." Once again, Leah had expressed that she didn't want Eve to be disappointed in her, although not in as many words.

"I'll go talk to her. I'll be back down soon."

Eve disappeared upstairs. Faith busied herself tidying up the lounge room while she waited. She and Eve would have to have a conversation about Leah soon, but with Eve so clearly worn down from work, now wasn't a good time. Which also meant their other serious conversation, about the events of the morning, might have to wait too.

When Eve returned, she collapsed onto the couch next to Faith. "Christ, this has been a long day."

"Want to talk about it?" Faith asked.

"Well, aside from things at work getting busy, Harrison is being difficult. I'm taking the twins to see my parents in England next week, and he's up in arms about me leaving the country with them. He wants to get his lawyers involved." Eve threw her hands up. "He spent most of the twins' lives barely acknowledging their existence, and suddenly he wants to be a father to them. And now this with Leah. She's upset about something, but she refuses to tell me what. Did she say anything to you?"

Faith hesitated. "Not specifically."

"What is it?" Eve asked.

"I have an idea of why she's upset, but I don't know if it's my place to say anything."

"Go ahead. I won't hold it against you."

Faith chose her words carefully. "Leah, she feels like she's under a lot of pressure from you."

"I suspected as much," Eve said. "It's true, I push her. I want her and Ethan to make the most of their potential, that's all."

"I think she feels like you put more pressure on her than Ethan. That you compare her to him. That you're disappointed in her when she doesn't measure up to her brother."

Eve was silent for a moment. "That's not how I feel. Not at all. I didn't know Leah felt that way. She's never said anything to me."

"Well, she didn't say it to me in those words. But she sees that you push her harder than Ethan, and she's afraid of disappointing you."

"I never meant for this to happen." Eve rubbed her temples with her fingertips. "It's true. I've always put more pressure on Leah than Ethan. But it's for her own good. I want her to be able to choose her own future."

"And she'll be able to do that. You're giving Leah and Ethan every opportunity a child could possibly have."

"It's not just about opportunities. I need to make sure that Leah has all the tools she needs to do whatever she wants with her life. Ethan, his future is already secure. Harrison is grooming him to be the heir to his company and his family fortune. Even if Ethan doesn't want to follow in his father's footsteps, his status will open every door for him. But Leah? If Harrison and his family have their way, there's only one path for her, and it's a narrow one. They expect her to grow up, get married, pop out children, and be the perfect housewife, living only to serve her husband. Just like they expected of Harrison's sisters. Just like they expected of me."

Faith knew what that was like. Her own family had expected the same thing of her.

"If that's what Leah wants, that's fine," Eve said. "But I don't want her growing up thinking that's her only option. I want her to know that there are other paths she can take. I want to put her in a position where she can succeed in spite of her father and his family. I need Leah to know that she can build a fulfilling life for herself, one that doesn't revolve around her family. And I need her to know that she's not less than the men in her life."

A pained expression crossed Eve's face. "Everything I've done, all the pressure I've been putting on her, was so she wouldn't grow up thinking she's lesser. Instead, I've made her think she doesn't measure up to her brother. I need to fix this. I can't have her growing up believing she's a disappointment. I'll talk to her. Apologize. Lay off her a little, especially with the extra schoolwork. Clearly, it's making her miserable. Who knows what that will do to her grades?"

"Leah's already ahead of most kids her age. And she has lots of other talents too. Her violin teacher is impressed with her progress. He says she has a gift for music."

"Really? I haven't heard her play in a long time." Eve sighed. "I suppose it's because I'm never home these days. Juggling work and the kids, it isn't easy."

"Don't forget you have help," Faith said.

"I do. The best help I could ask for."

Eve gave Faith a small smile before folding her hands in her lap, her expression growing serious. Faith knew that face. It meant business.

"We should talk about this morning," Eve said.

"Right." Faith had been afraid to bring it up.

"Truthfully, I've been so busy today that I haven't had a chance to think everything through."

"Maybe it's better that way," Faith said. "Not thinking about it. Just doing what you feel."

"That's easy for you to say. My situation is complicated." Eve crossed her legs. "I've been separated from Harrison for a few years now, but our divorce was only finalized recently. We weren't on good terms when we separated, and we both brought lots of assets to the marriage, so it took a long time to untangle everything. We're still in the middle of this custody battle. I'm on the verge of convincing Harrison to give me primary custody of the twins, but he's unwilling to compromise on anything else. His lawyers are sharks. They won't hesitate to use any ammunition they can find to paint me as an unfit mother. And they already have plenty of that."

Eve, an unfit mother? The idea was crazy. What could Harrison possibly have on Eve to suggest that?

But Eve didn't elaborate. "So, I need to be on my best behavior. And my lawyers have advised me that it's in my best interests to avoid dating and relationships until the custody situation is resolved. And under no circumstances am I to bring a lover or partner around the children. I need to be able to show I can provide the twins with a stable home environment, and I need to demonstrate that my children are my priority, not my romantic life. Being involved with someone so soon after the divorce will really hurt my case. Having a relationship with my children's nanny, a woman who works for me, is not a good look."

"Oh." Faith stifled her disappointment. "I understand. I wouldn't want to make things any harder for you."

"On the other hand, I've spent most of my adult life being on my best behavior. Being that perfect wife and mother that everyone demanded I be. I'm tired of it." Something sparked behind Eve's eyes. "And I'm very good at being discreet."

Faith smiled. "So am I."

Eve leaned in closer and brought her hand up to Faith's cheek. Faith thought Eve was going to kiss her. Instead, she asked a simple question.

"What do you want from me, Faith?"

"I... don't know." Faith chewed her lip in thought. "When I saw you at Lilith's Den, it was like something inside me awakened. But I don't know what that something is."

"You said the other night that you hadn't been able to stop thinking about me. The 'woman in the corset.'"

"Yes." Now it seemed so silly to think of that side of Eve as a whole other person.

"When you thought about that woman, what did you want from her?" Eve asked. "What appealed to you about her?"

"I think it was about what she represented. An idea." Faith paused. She didn't know how to put it into words.

"Surrender?" Eve said.

Was that what it was? Was that what Faith wanted?

"I can show you what that's like," Eve said. "That surrender. But you'll have to show me that you can give me your submission in return."

Faith nodded. "I can do that."

A smile crossed Eve's lips. "We'll find out if that's true very soon."

CHAPTER TEN

Can you go to the house? Eve's message read. *I need you to do something for me.*

Faith pried herself up from her couch and stretched out her arms. Eve and the twins were somewhere in the English countryside, visiting Eve's parents who had moved there years ago. Faith was taking full advantage of her time off. She'd spent the day at home doing absolutely nothing. But apparently Eve needed her, and she wouldn't ask if it wasn't important.

After replying to Eve's message, Faith got into her car and drove to the house. It was late evening, and the roads were clear. She arrived in record time.

As soon as she walked through the front door, her phone rang. *Eve.*

Faith picked it up. "I'm at the house."

"I know," Eve said. "The camera in the doorbell."

"Right." Faith had forgotten about it. "What do you need me to do?"

"First, I need you to go to my bedroom. I'll wait."

The other end of the line fell silent. Faith headed to Eve's bedroom. Even with Eve's permission, she felt an anxious thrill going into her boss's room.

"I'm in your bedroom," Faith said.

"I should let you know, there's a camera in the room," Eve said. "Hidden in the alarm clock."

Faith looked at the small clock on the nightstand. It looked like a regular alarm clock. She wouldn't have known it was a camera if Eve hadn't told her. Had it been in the room when Faith went into Eve's closet that day? Had Eve watched Faith snoop through her clothes?

Eve read Faith's mind. "I got it after an incident with a nosy babysitter, but I could never bring myself to use it. Spying on the help just seems wrong. But before I left for my trip I thought of a much more creative use for my nannycam."

Before Faith could ask what she meant, Eve gave her another command.

"Go into the closet and look to your left."

Faith entered Eve's walk-in closet. Hanging from a velvet coat hanger by the door was a baby doll chemise. It was made of sheer white fabric that was so fine and light it was almost transparent.

"Do you see it?" Eve asked.

"Yes," Faith said. "What do you want me to do?"

"Put it on."

"Now? Why?"

"Because my parents have taken the twins out for the evening. Right now, I'm all alone in the house, with nothing to do," Eve said. "I need some entertainment. You're going to put on a show for me."

It all clicked in Faith's mind. The camera. The lingerie. Warmth crept up her body. This was *not* the kind of task she expected to be doing for Eve this evening. Faith certainly wasn't complaining. Since the other night, when she and Eve had resolved to keep everything between them a secret, they'd barely had a moment alone. An illicit kiss here and there was all they'd been able to manage. Those fleeting kisses had only made Faith want Eve so much more.

She peered out at the room, her eyes falling on the hidden camera on the nightstand. "You're watching me?"

"Not yet," Eve said. "I want you to get ready first. Then the fun will begin."

Faith smiled. "What kind of fun?"

"So many questions." Faith could almost hear Eve shaking her head through the phone. "I told you you'd have to show me that you can submit to me. That you can obey my instructions. That you can surrender control. That is, if you still want that."

"Yes," Faith said. "I do."

"Then you're going to do exactly as I say. Now, put on the lingerie. And nothing else."

Faith put down the phone and slipped out of her jeans and t-shirt. When she was down to her panties, she took the chemise off the hanger. The delicate fabric was weightless in her hands. It was extremely short, and it didn't come with a pair of panties.

Heat rose through her. She stripped off her panties and slipped into the chemise, then turned to look at herself in the full-length mirror. The chemise only fell a few inches past her hipbones, barely enough to cover her. Through the sheer fabric, she could see the outlines of her nipples and the triangle of neatly trimmed hair at the apex of her thighs. Eve would be able to see everything.

Here goes nothing.

"I'm done," Faith said.

"Go back into the bedroom and put the camera at the end of the bed," Eve said. "Put your phone on speaker while you're at it."

Faith did as she was told. "Are you watching now?"

"Not yet. There are a few more things I need you to do first. Do you see the drawers under the bed?"

"Yes." The king-sized bed had several drawers built into the frame underneath the mattress for storage. Up close, Faith could see that they had locks on them.

"You'll need the key," Eve said. "It's in the bottom drawer of the dresser."

Faith went over to the dresser and retrieved the key. "Got it." She was starting to feel like she was on some kind of scavenger hunt.

"Open the first drawer on the right-hand side of the bed," Eve said. "Inside, you'll find a long box made of wood."

Faith unlocked the drawer and pulled it open. Sure enough, there was a long, thin box made of dark wood. And scattered in the velvet-lined drawer next to it were a dozen whips and canes, all of different lengths and sizes.

Faith stared. All of this had been in the house, right under her nose, the entire time she'd been working here?

How had she ever thought Eve was this boring, proper woman?

Faith glanced at the locked drawer next to it. There were even more drawers on the other side of the bed. Did they all contain kinky toys too?

"What's taking you so long?" Eve asked. "I hope you're not snooping."

"I'm not," Faith said. "I've found the box."

"Open it."

Faith placed the box on the bed. Inside was a long metal bar with a leather cuff attached to each end. "What's this?"

"You can't figure that out for yourself?"

It was obvious that it was some kind of restraint, but the cuffs were too big for Faith's wrists. Not that she'd be able to cuff her wrists by herself. And the bar was so long.

Oh. "These are for my ankles," Faith said.

"That's right," Eve said. "It's a spreader bar. Get onto the bed and put it on."

Faith climbed onto the bed and sat down in the center of it. The bed was so vast and soft that she felt like it was swallowing her up. She positioned her phone on the pillow and set about cuffing her ankles.

Once she had the first cuff on, she understood why it was called a 'spreader bar'. The long bar between the two cuffs would hold her legs wide apart. With nothing underneath the chemise Faith wore, Eve would have quite the view.

"Are you done?" Eve asked.

"Almost." Faith fastened the second cuff around her ankle. It wasn't easy. With her legs held apart, she had to stretch to her limits to reach her ankle.

When she was finished, she pulled the chemise down, covering as much of herself as she could. She wasn't shy. She simply wanted to draw things out, to reveal herself slowly to Eve. Eve wanted a show?

Faith would give her a show.

"I'm done," she said.

Eve's voice rang out from the phone next to her. "Then it's time to begin."

"Are you watching now?"

"I am. It's amazing how advanced technology is these days. I can see you as clearly as if I was in the room with you."

A thrill raced through Faith's body. "Do you like what you see?"

"I do." Eve's voice fell to a whisper. "That lingerie looks lovely on you. You have no idea how hot this makes me, seeing you in something I gave you, all laid out for me on my bed."

Faith bit her lip. Eve's sultry voice set off a thirst within her. "What do you need me to do for you, Eve? I'll do anything you want."

Eve chuckled softly. "Careful. You have no idea what goes on in the depths of my imagination. There are so many wicked things I'd love to do to you. For now, we're going to start with something simple."

Faith glanced at the phone, eagerly awaiting Eve's command.

"Do you ever touch yourself?" Eve asked. "Make yourself come?"

"You mean—" Faith's face grew hot. "Yes. Sometimes."

"Sometimes? When?"

"At night. Before I go to sleep."

"I want you to show me how you play with yourself when you're all alone. Show me what you do late at night, under the covers."

"Right now?" Although Faith had long gotten over the

puritanical beliefs that came with her upbringing, she still had this visceral reaction to being told to do something so taboo. Was this why she found Eve and these twisted games so exhilarating?

"Yes," Eve said. "But start slow. I enjoy a bit of foreplay."

There hadn't been any foreplay between them that night in the library at the party. Just the memory of it was enough to spur Faith to begin.

Laying back against the pillows, Faith skimmed a hand up one thigh, trailing her fingers all the way up to her chest. The chemise was so thin it was like she was touching her skin. She drew her fingertips up her breast. The way the delicate fabric rubbed against her nipples made them threaten to harden. She slipped her hand into the top of the chemise.

"I want to see you," Eve said. "Pull the chemise down."

Faith took the straps of the chemise and slid them from her shoulders. The flimsy cups fell down, her breasts bared for Eve to see.

"That's better," Eve said. "Keep going."

Faith brushed her hair back and let her hand continue down her neck. Her other hand wandered over her breasts. She made sure to look straight into the camera, emphasizing the sensuality of her movements. She was putting on a show, after all. This was for Eve's benefit, not for hers.

But as Faith swept her hands over her body, she recalled how Eve's fingers had felt on her skin, how Eve's touch had been tender yet demanding at the same time. An ache grew deep in her core. Completely unbidden, her hand crept down her stomach, past her belly button.

"Yes," Eve said. "Make yourself come for me."

Faith took the hem of the chemise and drew it up to her waist. With the spreader bar holding her legs apart, Eve could surely see how obscenely wet Faith was.

Eve's voice rose from the bed beside Faith. "From now on, every part of you belongs to me, including that pretty pussy of yours."

Faith sucked in a breath. She never thought she'd hear the word 'pussy' come out of Eve's mouth. Then again, she never thought she'd be lying on Eve's bed with her legs strapped apart.

She slid her fingers down her slit. Her folds were so hot they seemed to burn.

"Show me what you like," Eve said. "How you like to be touched."

Faith drew a finger up to her clit and traced slow spirals around it. Her other hand stayed up at her chest, tweaking her nipples. Her eyes fell closed as she sank into Eve's bed. It usually took her a long time to get warmed up, but knowing that Eve was watching her had her throbbing in no time at all.

"Do you wish that was me touching you right now?" Eve asked. "Me in the room with you?"

"Yes," Faith said. "More than anything."

"Pretend, for a moment, that I'm there. Imagine those are my hands on you. Show me what you want me to do with you."

Faith slid her hand down and dipped a finger inside herself, then another, easing them back and forth.

"Are you imagining that's me inside you?" Eve asked. "Just like at the party that night?"

"Yes," Faith said. "It felt incredible." She shifted in the

bed, raising her hips, letting the heel of her palm grind against her clit while her fingers curled inside her. Her legs trembled, fighting the spreader bar holding them apart.

"If I was really there with you, it wouldn't just be that spreader bar you'd be wearing," Eve said. "I'd tie your hands up too, so you'd have no choice but to let me have my fun with you."

An involuntary wave of heat rolled through her. Faith pumped her hand harder. Just minutes ago, she'd thought she was the one running the show, with her submissive words and sensual motions. There was no doubt now who commanded Faith's body. She was completely in Eve's thrall.

And it felt so good.

"You're close, aren't you?" Eve asked.

"Yes," Faith whispered. Could Eve really tell from the other side of the camera?

"Go on. Come for me."

Eve barely finished her sentence before Faith's pleasure peaked. She convulsed on the bed, Eve's name on her lips, her body overcome with an orgasm that stretched on and on until she came apart.

She fell back down to the pillows, breathing hard. Faintly, she could hear Eve's breaths through the phone.

After a moment, Eve cleared her throat. "Well, that certainly was entertaining. I asked for a show, and you delivered."

Faith murmured something senseless, her head full of fog.

"Sounds like you need to recover. Take all the time you want. And that lingerie? You can keep it."

"Really?" It had to be more expensive than any lingerie Faith owned. Or any other clothing she owned, for that matter.

"Consider it a gift. The matching panties too. They're in a bag in the closet. But since I didn't get to see them on you, I expect you to send me a photo of yourself wearing them later."

Faith grinned. "Okay. Thank you."

"I should go," Eve said. "Everyone will be back soon. And after the performance you just put on for me, I'm going to need a few more minutes of alone time."

Faith flushed all over. The thought of Eve pleasuring herself while thinking of her was almost enough to make Faith start touching herself again.

"I'll see you next week," Eve said. "Before you leave, make sure you put everything away and lock up the drawer."

Faith resisted the urge to roll her eyes in case Eve was still watching. Despite everything that had passed between them, Eve was still her usual bossy self.

Faith hung up the phone and took off the spreader bar, then carefully returned it to its drawer under the bed. Her eyes fell to the collection of whips. Now, they didn't look so intimidating. A picture of Eve wielding one sprung up in her mind. What would those whips feel like against her skin?

She shut the drawer, locked it up and got dressed. She was starting to see the appeal of giving up control. It was so addictive. Faith wanted more.

And she didn't know how to feel about that.

CHAPTER ELEVEN

Lindsey waved her hand in front of Faith's face. "Earth to Faith."

"Hm?" Faith shook herself out of her trance. She and Lindsey were sprawled out on the bed in one of the guest suites in Lindsey's mansion. Eve was still in England, and by coincidence, Lindsey's girlfriend was also out of town, so she'd invited Faith to stay overnight. Their days of sharing a college dorm were long gone, but every now and then they slept over at each other's houses like they were roommates again.

"Sorry," Faith said. "I have a lot on my mind right now."

Lindsey sat up. "Worried about your sister?"

"Yeah." That was one of the things that was troubling Faith. "I still haven't heard anything from her. I just hope nothing bad has happened."

"I'm sure she's fine." Lindsey gave her a sympathetic smile. "Maybe she's just busy. Or the letter got lost."

"Maybe." Her words did little to reassure Faith. Everything with Faith's family was far too complicated for Lindsey to understand. Although Faith had told her friend all about her past life, anyone who hadn't lived that life could never fully grasp the situation.

There was one person Faith could talk to who would understand. Her aunt. She was like Faith, having broken off from her family and their religion years before Faith did. When Faith had left home, it was her aunt Hannah who had taken her in. Other than her sister, Hannah was the only real family Faith still had a connection to. She made a mental note to call her later.

Faith's phone buzzed. It was a message from Eve. She opened it up.

I'm stuck at the world's dullest dinner party. To pass the time, I'm thinking about how you looked on my bed in that lingerie.

A rush went through her. She and Eve had been exchanging messages for days now, each racier than the last. Every one of them made Faith ache with desire.

But at the same time, doubt gnawed at her. It didn't make sense that she wanted this. To submit to Eve, to give Eve so much power over her. For most of Faith's life, she'd felt so powerless, trapped in a world where she didn't have any control or agency, where she was expected to be this dutiful, subservient woman. She'd chosen to leave that life behind years ago. How was she supposed to reconcile that with her newly discovered submissive desires?

"You're zoning out again," Lindsey said.

"Right. Sorry." Faith put her phone down. "I just got a message from Eve."

Lindsey grinned. "I'm guessing it wasn't about a nannying emergency?"

"Nope."

"So things are going well between the two of you?"

"Mostly." Faith had filled Lindsey in on what was going on between herself and Eve, with the caveat that she couldn't tell anyone, not even Camilla. "It's just that, I've never been with someone who's into the things Eve is. I have some reservations."

Lindsey frowned. "Do you feel pressured to do things you don't want to? Because I know you're new to all this, but consent is important in these kinds of relationships."

"No, that's not it. We've talked about that stuff." In between exchanging risqué messages, Faith and Eve had talked about their boundaries. Faith had told Eve in no uncertain terms was Eve to put her in a cage. "It's not the physical stuff. It's everything else."

"What do you mean?"

"It's about how all this makes me feel. How *she* makes me feel. I want her. I want to explore this submissive side of myself with her. And it bothers me that I want that." Faith sat up on the bed and crossed her legs underneath her. "I spent most of my life having everything about me controlled, from what I wore, to what I did with my life. And since I escaped that life, I've always been wary of people trying to control me. Friends, partners, anyone." She balled her fists in her lap. "I don't ever want to feel like I'm someone's property. Never again."

"Does Eve make you feel that way?" Lindsey asked.

"I don't think so. It's different with her. But maybe that's just because I'm blinded by everything I feel for her."

"Or maybe it's because, with Eve, it *is* different. What you're doing with her, it's not the same as being controlled.

That's not to say it's not real, or it's just a game. The difference is that submission is a choice. You're not having power taken away from you. You're giving it to someone willingly. And there's nothing wrong with wanting to do that." Lindsey folded her arms on her chest. "Look at Camilla and me. Do you think there's anything unhealthy about our relationship?"

"No." Faith had to admit, she'd been skeptical of Lindsey and Camilla's relationship in the beginning. The two of them had jumped headfirst into this intense, 24/7 kinky relationship. But after witnessing the two of them together for a year now, it was clear to Faith that what they had was healthy and loving. It was all give and take, and they were equals where it really mattered.

"It still feels wrong for *me* to want that," Faith said. "I know it's silly, but I feel like it goes against all my principles. I fought to escape a life of submission and servitude, so I could become a modern woman, independent and strong."

"I get it. I've felt that way before too. Eventually, I realized that my desires don't reflect who I am as a person. Although they're a part of me, they don't define me. And they aren't a weakness."

"I guess that makes sense."

"Besides, that's what makes submission so appealing."

"What do you mean?" Faith asked

"Submission lets you explore a side of yourself you don't get to let out in the real world. That vulnerable side of yourself. It lets you feel things you're not supposed to feel, want things you're not supposed to want. But it's about more than just the thrill of the forbidden. It's about letting go of all the ideas you have about yourself and giving in to desire.

And when you reach that point where you can let go of everything and just exist in the moment with that special person? It's so freeing." Lindsey brushed back her auburn hair. "Of course, it takes a long time to reach that place with someone. And it takes trust. But that's ultimately what it's all about. That surrender."

There it was again. That word. *Surrender.* The idea appealed to Faith. Was that what she wanted?

She groaned. "This is all too complicated."

"It doesn't have to be," Lindsey said. "Do you remember when Camilla and I first got together? Someone wise told me that I should stop worrying about what I thought I should and shouldn't feel and just let myself feel it. Maybe you should take her advice."

It was just like Lindsey to throw Faith's words back at her. "That was different."

"Was it?"

Faith sighed. "Maybe you're right."

"Of course, that same someone thought it was a good idea for us to go skinny dipping in the lake next to campus in the middle of the night, so maybe she isn't that wise."

Faith rolled her eyes. "That was years ago."

"God, it was, wasn't it? It still feels like yesterday."

Faith flopped back down on the bed. Lindsey was right. She had no reason to be ashamed of what she felt. She had to embrace it.

She was not powerless.

Submission was a choice.

And she chose to submit to Eve.

Faith picked up her phone and typed out a reply to Eve's

message. *I liked being bound on your bed for you. I just wish you'd been there to tie me up yourself.*

Eve's response was instantaneous.

When I get back, I'm going to tie you to my bed and do all those wicked things I've been dreaming about doing to you.

CHAPTER TWELVE

Faith unlocked the front door and strode into the house. "Eve? I'm back."

"In here," Eve replied.

Faith followed Eve's voice toward the living room, anticipation burning inside of her. Eve and the twins had returned from their vacation the day before, and Faith had returned to work this morning, but she and Eve hadn't had a moment alone.

Not until now.

Eve met Faith outside the living room. "You're back." She removed her glasses and slipped them into her pocket. "The twins are at school?"

"Just dropped them off," Faith replied.

"Good. We have the house to ourselves."

Without warning, Eve drew Faith in for an urgent, fiery kiss. A blissful hum rose from Faith's chest. The kiss drew out, Eve's lips growing hungrier and hungrier, filling Faith with a deep, aching need.

Eve broke away. "I have half an hour before I have to leave for work. That should give us enough time."

"For what?" Faith asked.

Eve pushed Faith hard against the wall and leaned close, speaking into her ear. "For me to make you come like you did for me on camera."

Faith's breath quickened. Who was this crazed woman who had taken over Eve's body? Faith wasn't complaining at all.

Eve pressed her lips against Faith's again, suffocating her. Faith grabbed onto the collar of Eve's blouse, holding herself up in the face of Eve's onslaught. Eve pulled the bottom of Faith's blouse out of her skirt, her hand creeping up underneath Faith's bra. At the same time, Faith began unbuttoning Eve's blouse. Eve had seen Faith in nothing but lingerie, but Faith hadn't seen so much as a bare patch of Eve's skin.

Eve drew away, shaking her head. "When are you going to learn that I'm the one running the show?" She took Faith's wrists and pinned them to the wall. "Keep your hands to yourself."

Faith nodded. She was so desperate for Eve's touch that she would have done anything Eve told her to do.

Eve released Faith's hands so she could lift up the hem of Faith's skirt. She yanked it up past Faith's hips, eliciting a gasp from Faith. Eve wasn't wasting any time. Faith flattened her palms against the wall to keep herself from touching Eve. It was sweet torture.

Eve drew back, her head cocked. "Do you hear that?"

"What?" Faith listened carefully. The faint sound of a key in the front door reached her ears.

Eve cursed. "Someone's here. Quick, go into the kitchen."

Faith pulled down her skirt and hurried into the kitchen. As she shut the door, she caught a glimpse of Eve hastily buttoning up her shirt and heard the sound of heavy footsteps in the hall.

"What are you doing here?" Eve's voice. "You can't barge in like this."

"Will you relax?" A man's voice this time. "I didn't think you'd be home."

"How did you get in here, Harrison?"

Harrison. Eve's ex-husband. Faith pressed her ear to the kitchen door, her curiosity getting the best of her. Eve rarely spoke of Harrison, but when she did, it was with palpable disdain. What had happened between them to make Eve despise him so fiercely?

"I still have a key," Harrison said.

Eve huffed. "I'm changing the locks."

"No need. If it's such a big deal, you can have it back."

"It is a big deal!" Eve's voice rose. "You can't just let yourself into my house."

"Whose money do you think bought this house?"

"Don't start with that again."

"What?" Harrison said. "It's true."

"It's not like you don't have a dozen other houses. This house is the only thing I took in the divorce. Given all the sacrifices I made for the children, it's far less than I deserve."

"Those sacrifices were your choice."

Eve scoffed. "We both know I didn't really have a choice. Not with you and Eleanor constantly manipulating me."

Eve had mentioned Eleanor's name at the party that night. She was Harrison's mother.

"Settle down," Harrison said. "I'm not having this argument with you again."

Eve said something too quietly for Faith to make out, but she was certain it wasn't polite. She was beginning to understand why Eve felt so much contempt toward her ex-husband. He spoke to Eve like she was a child.

"Why did you come here?" Eve asked.

"I need Ethan's baseball gear," Harrison replied. "I have him this afternoon, remember? I'm taking him to the park after school."

"You should have called me."

"I thought you'd be at work. I didn't think you'd mind."

"I do mind," Eve said.

"Clearly. I said I was sorry."

"No, you didn't."

"Fine," Harrison said. "I'm sorry."

Faith's nose began to itch. *No. Not now.* She covered her face with her hands and screwed up her nose, just in time to muffle the sneeze. But it wasn't enough.

"What was that?" Harrison asked.

"The nanny," Eve replied. "She's doing some chores for me."

"I still don't see why you need a nanny."

"I have a job now. Looking after the kids is a lot of work. Not that you'd know anything about that."

"If someone else is going to be raising my kids, I want to meet her," Harrison said.

Eve's voice grew icy. "She's not raising our kids. *I* am.

And you're one to talk. Whenever it's your time with them, it's Eleanor who looks after them."

"At least she's family and not some stranger."

"Faith isn't a stranger. And the children love her."

"Then let me meet her," Harrison said.

"Fine. Just don't be an ass. I know that's difficult for you, but at least try."

Eve's footsteps approached the kitchen. Faith hastily tucked in her blouse.

"Faith?" Eve opened the door. "Will you come out here, please? Harrison would like to meet you." She brought her hand up to smooth down Faith's hair and gave her an apologetic grimace.

Steeling herself, Faith followed Eve out into the hall.

"Faith, this is Harrison," Eve said through gritted teeth. "My ex-husband."

Harrison flashed Faith a smile. "Harrison Mathers."

He held out his hand for Faith to shake. His grip was firm and practiced, as if he spent all day shaking hands. From his suit to his stance, everything about him seemed meticulously crafted to project an image of the perfect man.

"Eve doesn't have you working too hard, does she?" Harrison asked. "I know the twins can be a handful."

"Don't pretend you actually know what parenting them is like," Eve muttered.

"The twins are great," Faith said. "They're easy kids."

Eve put her hands on her hips. "There, now you've met the nanny." She turned to Faith. "Would you bring Ethan's baseball gear down? It's in his room."

"Sure," Faith replied.

As Faith walked up the stairs, Eve and Harrison continued their conversation in hushed voices. Faith couldn't hear a word. By the time she returned with Ethan's baseball bag, they had fallen silent, tension hanging heavy in the air.

Faith handed Harrison the bag. He slung it over his shoulder.

"I need to get to work soon," Eve said.

"Hint taken. Here." Harrison dropped a key into Eve's hand. "I'll see you at the next pickup." With a nod of farewell, he sauntered back down the hall.

Eve glared at him until he was out the door. "That was close. The last thing I need is for Harrison to find us together."

"Right," Faith said. "The custody situation."

"Yes. I'm not supposed to be seeing anyone, especially not my nanny. I have no doubt his lawyers will crucify me if they find out. I don't want to make their job any easier than it already is."

What was that supposed to mean? It wasn't the first time Eve had implied Harrison's lawyers had some kind of dirt on her.

Eve pocketed the key. "Besides, these are two worlds that are never meant to collide."

"What do you mean?" Faith asked.

"I mean the 'me' who has two kids, an ex-husband, and goes to PTA meetings is a different person than the woman you saw at Lilith's Den. It's no coincidence you barely recognized me that night. It's deliberate, the way I express myself there. It's a way to keep those parts of myself separate."

"Why do you want to keep them separate?"

"It's simpler that way."

Faith thought back to her conversation with Lindsey. About how submission was about letting go, giving in to one's deepest desires. Was the same true in reverse? Was Eve seeking the same surrender that Faith was?

"And now I have a more practical reason to keep those worlds separate," Eve said. "I don't want anyone to catch wind of the two of us. We need to be more careful, especially with the twins in the picture. And we need to set some boundaries. No more of this in the house. We should have avoided that from the start. Whenever you're here, I'm your employer, and that's it."

"All right." Faith didn't want to put Eve's family at risk. But she didn't want things between them to end. "Can we still send each other messages? I like your messages."

"Sure." Eve's lips curled up into a smile. "I need some way to keep you on your toes until we get the chance to have some private time together."

Faith's cheeks flushed. "So, how are we going to do that? Have time together without anyone discovering us?"

"It won't be easy, but we'll manage. All this means is that we're going to have to get a lot more creative from now on."

CHAPTER THIRTEEN

Faith got off the elevator at the floor of Eve's office. The twins were at their father's, so Eve had opted to work late. She'd called Faith an hour ago, asking her to drop off a flash drive she'd forgotten at home.

Faith was greeted at the reception desk by Andrea. The receptionist was packing up to leave.

"Go right in," she said. "Ms. Lincoln is expecting you."

Faith thanked her and headed into the office. It was late evening, but there were still a handful of people around. It seemed Eve worked her employees just as hard as she worked Faith.

She knocked on the door to Eve's office.

"Come in," Eve said.

Faith entered the room and shut the door behind her. Eve was sitting behind her desk again, focused intently on her laptop.

Eve looked up at Faith. "You have the drive?"

Faith nodded. "Here it is."

Eve took the drive and plugged it into her laptop, scanning the screen. "This is the one. Once again, you're a lifesaver. Thank you."

"No problem. Is there anything else I can do for you?"

Eve tilted her head to the side, a slight smile forming on her lips. "Now that you mention it, there *is* something else I could use your help with."

"Sure," Faith said. "Whatever you need."

Eve leaned back in her leather chair and folded her arms across her chest. "There you go again with your unwavering obedience. Didn't I warn you about that? If you're not careful, I might take you at your word. Do all those dirty things I've been dreaming about doing to you."

Faith dropped her eyes to escape Eve's piercing gaze. "I wouldn't mind if you did."

Eve let out a soft laugh. "You're just insatiable, aren't you? For now, I have a simple task for you. I've been working all day. I need to relax. Unwind."

"What do you have in mind?"

Eve peered at Faith over her glasses. "I could really use a massage."

Oh. Faith glanced around. Suddenly, the room felt stuffy.

"Why don't you lock the door?" Eve said.

Faith went over to the door and twisted the lock shut.

Eve fiddled with her phone on the desk in front of her. Classical music began playing from a speaker on her desk. "That's better," she said. "Makes the outside world simply fade away."

Eve shrugged her jacket off her shoulders and folded it on the desk next to her. Then, she began unbuttoning her blouse, slowly exposing the smooth white skin of her chest and the lacy black bra she wore underneath. It was thin and low cut, her breasts appearing to spill out of them. Faith stared, her lips parting.

Eve slipped off her shirt and folded it on top of her jacket on the desk, then beckoned Faith with a finger. "Come stand behind my chair."

Faith rounded the desk to stand behind Eve. Eve drew the straps of her bra down her shoulders.

"Go on," she said. "Don't be afraid to use a little pressure."

Pushing aside her growing desire, Faith placed her hands on Eve's shoulders. Her skin was supple and warm. Faith began rubbing her thumbs in firm circles at the base of Eve's neck, working her way outward and over her shoulders. Her muscles loosened under Faith's fingertips.

Eve let out a satisfied groan. "God yes."

Faith kneaded Eve's shoulders even harder. Eve wasn't lying about being tense. But the sounds coming from Eve's mouth were so sensual. And touching her like this, skin to skin, was more than they'd touched in days. Was Eve trying to get Faith all hot and bothered?

Because it was working.

"Yes, right there," Eve said. "Harder."

Faith pushed harder into Eve's shoulders, eliciting even more pleasured murmurs from Eve. It was like music to Faith's ears. She had dreamed of making Eve come apart, but in an altogether different way...

"I didn't ask you to stop," Eve said.

"Right. Sorry." Faith resumed her massage, banishing all sexy thoughts from her mind. But Eve seemed determined to torment her. As she peered down over Eve's head, one of the cups of Eve's bra slipped down, exposing a rose-colored nipple.

God, how Faith ached to run her fingers over those soft, round breasts of Eve's. To feel Eve against her, just like at the party that night, but this time without any clothing between them—

Eve swiveled in her chair to face Faith. "Is something distracting you?"

"No," Faith said. "Well, yes. You are." She shook herself. She was having a hard time forming sentences. "But in a good way."

"Maybe I can do something about that." She drew a hand up Faith's arm, a wicked look in her eyes. "Relieve all that pressure."

Blood rushed to Faith's face. It wasn't hard to figure out what Eve was suggesting. "Here? Now?"

"Here and now." Eve stood up. Her face was barely an inch from Faith's. The scent of Eve's perfume enveloped her. She could practically taste those lips she so longed to kiss. "Unless you have any objections."

"No," Faith said. "No objections."

Eve stepped aside and pointed to the chair. "Sit."

Faith bit back a protest. She didn't want to sit down. She wanted to kiss Eve, to hold her, to drown in her. But the hard look in Eve's eyes told her Eve meant business.

Faith sat down in Eve's chair. It smelled like leather and Eve. It did nothing to quell the urge to bury herself in the other woman.

Eve opened the bottom drawer of her desk. "I did say I was going to tie you to my bed sometime, but since the house is off-limits we'll have to improvise." Eve pulled something out of the drawer. "This will work nicely."

Faith looked at the small package in Eve's hand. It was a two-pack of pantyhose.

"I always keep spares at work. It pays to be prepared." Eve tore the package open and pulled out both pairs of pantyhose, stretching them between her hands like a rope. "Do you have a safeword?"

"Uh…" Faith's mind went blank. She'd never needed a safeword before.

"Let's go with something simple? Red. Red means stop."

Faith nodded. "Okay."

"Arms on the armrests," Eve commanded.

Faith did as she was told. Using the pantyhose, Eve tied one of Faith's wrists to the arm of the chair, then the other, securing them with a series of knots. Faith's pulse raced. The bonds weren't tight, but the way they were looped around the armrests meant she had no chance of slipping out of them. She wasn't getting out of this chair. Not by herself.

Eve picked up her phone and turned the music up even louder. "I'm in the habit of playing music when I'm here after hours. It helps me concentrate. Anyone still in the office will just think I'm working late too." She leaned down over Faith's chair, resting a hand on the backrest above Faith's shoulder. "It'll help cover up all those delightful little sounds I'm going to coax out of you."

Faith squirmed in her chair. Suddenly, the ties around her wrists felt extremely tight.

Eve drew her hand up the front of Faith's thigh, continuing up her stomach. Even through the dress Faith wore,

Eve's touch made her shiver. Eve traced the pads of her fingers between Faith's breasts and up to her collarbone, brushing them along it gently. Faith's skin sizzled under Eve's fingertips.

Eve tore down the top of Faith's dress and bra, exposing her breasts. The cool air made her nipples tighten. Eve pinched one lightly. Faith gasped, her head falling over the back of the chair.

Eve reached down, pulling Faith's loose dress up past her hips, then slipped her hand between Faith's legs, skimming her fingers down Faith's panties. They were getting wetter by the second. She ground the heel of her hand against the peak of Faith's thighs, stoking the fire between them.

"Eve." Faith lifted her hips out toward Eve's hand. "*Please.*"

"Oh, Faith," Eve purred. "How I love to hear you beg."

Eve grabbed the waistband of Faith's panties and ripped them down her legs, then tossed them onto the desk beside her. She planted her knee between Faith's thighs, forcing them apart again, then snaked her hand down, all the way to the top of Faith's slit.

Faith exhaled sharply. Eve pushed a finger between Faith's lips, rolling it over Faith's aching bud. Eve's touch was gentle and light, but Faith was already so turned on that Eve's teasing strokes sent ripples through her. Her arms twitched in her bonds. She longed to touch Eve, to pull her close, or even just to kiss her. With Eve leaning over her, her hot breath on Faith's cheek and her lips so close to Faith's, it was like she was dangling that kiss just out of reach.

Eve's eyes locked onto Faith's. "I've been waiting so long

to do this again. Ever since I watched you on camera that night."

Eve ran her fingers down to Faith's entrance. Faith shifted forward to the edge of the chair, lifting her hips. The position strained her shoulders, but she was so drunk with desire that she barely noticed.

"I was watching very carefully," Eve said. "Watching what you like. Watching what makes you moan."

Eve slid into her slowly, easing in and out. Faith shuddered, pleasure lancing through her. Her fingers still inside Faith, Eve pushed her thumb up to graze Faith's clit. A cry fell from Faith's lips. She pressed them together. There were still people in the office, right outside Eve's door. Was the music loud enough to drown out all the noises Faith was making?

Eve picked up the pace, thrusting and stroking harder and faster. Faith bit the inside of her cheek, trying her hardest to keep silent, but the thrill of Eve taking her in an office full of people only pushed her closer to the edge.

"Eve," she whimpered.

"You're going to have to come quietly," Eve said. "Can you do that?"

Faith screwed her eyes shut. "Yes."

Eve sped up her fingers. "Then come."

At once, the pleasure inside her burst, flooding her entire body. The scream that escaped her was barely drowned out by the music. She gripped the arms of the chair until the tremors racking her body subsided.

As Faith caught her breath, Eve snipped through the pantyhose that bound her wrists, freeing her, then drew

Faith up out of the chair and pulled her in close. Their lips met in a firm, insistent kiss.

A sigh rose from Faith's chest, her whole body singing. *Finally.* The deep kiss felt even better than an orgasm, and it was even more satisfying. Eve's lips were like honey to her starving body.

Eve pulled back. "I have one more job for you to do for me."

"Anything," Faith said.

Eve sat down in her chair and pushed it back from the desk. She pointed to the floor before her. "Get down on your knees."

Faith obeyed.

Eve reached down to tilt Faith's chin up toward her. "Now it's my turn to have a little fun." She dragged her free hand up her leg and slid her skirt up her thigh. "Do you want to taste me?"

"God, yes," Faith said.

Eve drew her skirt up around her waist and peeled down her pantyhose. Underneath, she wore a pair of black panties that matched her bra. She slipped out of her panties and placed them next to Faith's on the desk, before resting her arms on the armrests and sliding forward until her hips were at the edge of the chair.

Eve parted her legs. "Go on."

Faith let out a soft breath. Everything about Eve was so intoxicating. Her skin, her hair, her scent. What lay where her thighs met was no exception.

Slowly, Faith slid her hand up the inside of Eve's leg and up past her knee. The skin there was so soft. Eve spread her legs even further apart, her hand falling to where Faith's shoulder met her neck.

Faith leaned forward and parted Eve's lips with her fingertips, then pushed her tongue between them. She closed her eyes, savoring Eve's taste, exploring her folds with her mouth. The tip of her tongue found Eve's tiny pearl. She sucked it gently.

"Mm, god." Eve's grip on the side of Faith's neck tightened. "That feels incredible."

Faith reached up to anchor herself on the inside of Eve's thighs, licking and sucking fervently. A soft moan spilled from Eve's lips. Eve was holding back, keeping quiet so no one would hear them, but the way her body reacted to Faith's touch was uninhibited.

Faith let out a moan of her own. She couldn't help herself. She'd always found giving just as satisfying as receiving. She lost herself between Eve's legs, and in the sweet, muted sounds rising from her. The rest of the office faded away, along with the rest of the world. All that existed was the two of them. All that mattered was Eve.

Eve's thighs quivered around Faith's head. "Yes. I'm so close."

She rose up into Faith, her whole body shaking as she came hard and fast. Her mouth fell open, but she didn't make a sound. Faith didn't stop until Eve's hand slid limply from her neck.

Faith looked up at Eve. Her head was tipped over the back of her hair, her eyes glazed over.

"Get up here," she murmured.

Faith stood up, her knees aching and her legs tingling as blood rushed back into them. Eve grabbed Faith's arm and pulled her down onto her lap, planting a lazy, lingering kiss on her lips.

Faith smiled. "So, how did I do? Did that help you relax?"

"It certainly did." Eve then cupped Faith's cheek in her hand. "It makes me wish I didn't have to get back to work."

"Do you really have to?" Faith asked.

"I do. I didn't ask you to come here so I could get you out of your panties. That was a bonus. I really did forget that drive."

Reluctantly, Faith got up from Eve's lap. "And I'm glad you forgot it."

Eve planted a playful spank on Faith's ass cheek and handed over her panties. As Faith slipped into them, Eve put her blouse back on and straightened out the rest of her clothes.

She pulled Faith in for one last smoldering kiss, which drew on and on until Eve pushed Faith away. "I'll see you tomorrow," she said. "Don't be late."

Faith said goodbye and left Eve's office. There were still a few people around, so Faith tried her hardest not to betray the fact that she'd just had her mouth between their boss's thighs. Her head was still spinning from the thrill of it all.

And yet, it fell short of what Faith truly wanted from Eve. She was starting to understand what it was now, that elusive something she hadn't been able to articulate. She wanted more than these erotic games. She wanted to give Eve so much more, wanted Eve to take so much more of her.

She wanted true surrender, the kind that only Eve could give her.

CHAPTER FOURTEEN

Faith opened Leah's door a crack and peered through it. Just like Ethan, she was sound asleep. Eve had put them to bed ten minutes earlier before retiring to her office. She'd asked Faith to check on them before she left.

Faith shut Leah's door and headed downstairs. She was done for the day, but she didn't want to go home yet. She longed to steal a moment with Eve, even though they couldn't do anything but talk.

She sighed. That was how it was between them now. When they were in the house, they were strictly boss and employee. They had slipped a few times with a hurried kiss, or teasing touch, or whispered word. And every one of those moments filled Faith with an unquenchable thirst.

As she reached the bottom of the stairs, she heard a loud crash. It had come from the back of the house. Faith rushed down the hall, calling out Eve's name. Eve didn't answer her. But as she got closer, she heard Eve cursing from her office. Faith hurried toward the sound.

She found Eve standing in front of her desk. Faith breathed a sigh of relief. Eve was unhurt. However, everything that had been on top of the desk lay scattered across the floor, and Eve's face was clouded over with anger.

"Eve?" Faith entered the room tentatively. She'd never seen Eve like this before. "Is everything all right?"

"That bastard," Eve spat. "I can't believe he's doing this. He didn't even have the decency to tell me himself."

Faith didn't have to ask who 'he' was. There was only one man who Eve spoke of with such disdain. "What's happened?"

"I just got a phone call from my lawyer. Harrison's lawyer informed her that he's decided to petition for sole custody. He's trying to take the kids from me."

Faith's stomach dropped. "Eve, I'm so sorry."

"It's all because I went back to work and hired a nanny. He claims he's doing this because he doesn't want the twins to be raised by a stranger." The muscles in Eve's neck tightened. "He said I've abandoned my duties as a mother."

"That's not true at all." From the moment Faith had started working for her, it had been clear that Eve was dedicated to raising the twins herself. She had Faith take care of the practical things so she could take care of everything that mattered. Faith might be the one who took them to music lessons, but Eve made a point of going to all their recitals. It was Faith's job to get the twins ready for bed, but it was Eve who tucked them in and read them a bedtime story every single night. And since Eve and Faith's conversation about Leah, her attentiveness to the children's needs had only grown. Eve had followed through with her promise to stop pushing Leah so hard, and their relationship had only gotten stronger.

"The truth doesn't matter to him," Eve said. "And if he gets custody, it's not going to be him who raises them. They'll end up brought up by servants. Or worse, his mother, who will fill their heads with toxic ideas."

"You can fight this, can't you?" Faith asked.

"Of course. But this is going to be a dirty, drawn-out fight. He has the best lawyers money can buy. So do I, but my funds aren't infinite. Most of my money is in my firm. He has all his family supporting him, and you bet their ass they're going to help him." Eve's jaw set. "It's always been me against them. And now they've made it their mission to take the twins away from me."

"It'll be okay," Faith said. "You'll get through this."

"I can't lose the twins," Eve said. "They're my everything. Harrison knows that. And he knows that cutting me out of their lives isn't what's best for them. I know he does."

Faith felt a pang of sympathy. Although it had always been clear there was no love lost between Eve and Harrison, it seemed that Eve hadn't expected Harrison to do something so extreme.

"He wasn't always like this." Eve's voice took on a bitter tone. "When we met, back in college, he was different. Kinder. I had no reason to believe he'd turn out to be the man he was. His family was the same. When I first met them, they all seemed lovely, if not a little old-fashioned and traditional. All old-money families are like that. Mine is too, although my parents aren't as extreme as his. They supported me going to college and making a career for myself, even if they did expect me to get married and have children one day. I wanted that for myself too. I always wanted to be a mother, and in this day and age I thought I'd never have to choose between having children and a career."

Eve leaned back against her desk and crossed one ankle over the other. "But Harrison's family felt differently. As soon as we got married, they started pressuring us to have children. I wasn't ready back then. I'd finished business school, and I was moving up the ladder at my job, and I didn't want to jeopardize that. He supported me at first. But as time passed, his family wore him down and he started pressuring me too." She shook her head. "I should have seen that as the red flag it was. But slowly, they all began to wear me down. Eventually, I agreed to start a family with Harrison, just as long as it didn't mean giving up my career. Harrison knew that. He understood that. Or at least, I thought he did at the time."

Faith thought back to the conversation between the two of them that she'd eavesdropped on. Harrison hadn't seemed like the supportive type at all.

"The truth became clear when I was pregnant," Eve said. "I ended up in the hospital for several months with serious complications. I almost lost the twins at one point." Her voice wavered. "It was then that Harrison suggested that for the twins' sakes, I needed to give up my career and dedicate my life to raising them. I was so emotional over almost losing the twins that I agreed. And I convinced myself that it would be enough. That the twins, my family, would be enough. But it wasn't."

She looked at Faith, a hint of guilt in her eyes. "Don't get me wrong. I find being a mother so fulfilling. But I needed something more in my life to feel whole. So when the twins were old enough, I told Harrison I wanted to go back to work. He said no. I tried to compromise. Said I'd work part-time, and we could have his mother look after the twins or hire a nanny. But he outright forbade it. It should have been a wake-up call for me, but with everything I was going through, I couldn't see what was right in front of my face."

Eve trailed off. Faith could hear the pain in her words. Was there something more there? Something Eve couldn't bring herself to speak about?

"It took a while, but in the end, I came to my senses," Eve said. "I separated from Harrison temporarily, and after only a few weeks, I knew that I couldn't stay with him any longer, so I ended things. That was years ago, but the divorce dragged out, and this custody battle has just dragged out even longer. I thought our negotiations were finally getting somewhere, but this nightmare never ends."

"Oh Eve." Faith took Eve's hand in both of hers. "I'm so sorry you went through all that. And I'm sorry things are still this hard."

"I'm not sorry. There was one good thing that came out of it. Two actually. Leah and Ethan. I'd do it all again for them." Her hand tightened in Faith's. "I won't let Harrison take them. His family is capable of terrible things, and I won't let them get their claws into the twins. If they think I'm going to roll over, they're wrong. I'm going to fight this."

"And I'll be right here if you need me," Faith said. "Even if you just want to talk. I'm here for anything."

"Thank you. I appreciate it." Eve pushed herself up to sit on the top of her desk. "This all seems like a bad dream. I don't know what I'd do without the twins. For so long, my whole life, my whole identity, has been being a wife and mother."

"You're not going to lose the twins. And you're plenty of things besides a wife and a mother."

"I'm trying to be." Eve sighed. "I'm far too old to still be finding myself."

"I don't think finding yourself stops at a certain age." Faith sat on the desk next to her. "Isn't it just something we're all constantly trying to do?"

"Does that include you?" Eve asked.

"Of course."

Eve studied Faith. "You don't seem the type to worry about that kind of thing. Who you are. Your place in the world. Your purpose in life. You've always seemed so free-spirited. So carefree."

"I think about that stuff a lot. And I'm not carefree." If only Eve knew how much Faith had agonized over their secret relationship. "My identity is something I've struggled with my whole life. I grew up in a traditional, religious family. My parents, they expected me to be this devout, virtuous woman who followed all their rules, from what I wore, to who I'd marry one day." That was *who*, not *if*. Faith had never had a choice in the matter. "In the end, I just couldn't be this person they wanted me to be, so I left that life behind. I left my family behind." The reality was far more dramatic, but Faith didn't want to go into detail.

"That must have been difficult," Eve said.

"It was. But I got through it. And here I am." Faith looked at Eve. "I know what it's like, to be expected to live a life that isn't your own, to be shoved in a box you don't fit into. And I know how hard it is to try to move on from that, to figure out who you are when everything you know has been torn away from you. It's been almost eight years since then, and I'm still trying to figure myself out."

Eve gave her a soft smile. "We have more in common than I thought."

They sat in silence for a moment, shoulder to shoulder and hand in hand. It felt good to be able to support Eve in the tiniest way. For all their kinky games and dirty talk, Faith really cared about Eve. And after working for the family for so long now, Faith had come to know the twins so well too. Eve losing the twins, the twins losing their mother, would be a terrible outcome. It pained her to think of the turmoil Eve was in.

Eve looked down at the floor where the contents of her desktop were scattered. "I need to clean this up."

"I'll help," Faith said.

"No. This mess is because of my tantrum. I'll deal with it. You should go home. You've been here since morning."

"Okay. Let me know if you need anything."

"There is one thing," Eve said. "What Harrison is doing, it changes things. The stakes are higher now. It makes it even more important that I be on my best behavior. We can't have anyone finding out about us now. What we did in my office was far too risky."

"You're right." Faith felt a tightness in her chest. "If things between us are causing problems for you, maybe we should stop."

Eve shook her head. "That's not what I want. We just need to be even more careful about keeping everything under wraps."

Faith felt a wave of relief. "Okay." Although she was glad

to take a step back if it made things easier for Eve, the thought of giving up on what the two of them had made her heart ache.

"Fortunately, we still have options when it comes to seeing each other," Eve said. "There's a place we can go where no one will ever dare to out us."

"Where's that?" Faith asked.

Eve smiled. "How do you feel about a night at Lilith's Den?"

CHAPTER FIFTEEN

Faith held up a slinky black dress in front of herself in the mirror. She frowned. It was too plain. She needed something more daring. More risqué.

She tossed it onto her bed and started rifling through her closet again. In just a few hours, she and Eve were returning to Lilith's Den. They were finally going to get a chance to be together openly. Eve had told Faith that there was an unwritten rule in the BDSM community, that outing anyone was unforgivable. The rules of Lilith's Den added that extra layer of privacy. What happened at Lilith's stayed at Lilith's.

Faith let out a wistful sigh. They were going back to the place where it all began for her. The place that had awakened Faith to all kinds of unexpected pleasures. The place where Faith had discovered a side of her boss that she never expected.

But that wasn't all that made tonight special. Up until now, everything between her and Eve had felt like a game.

So far, Faith had only dipped her toes into the world of submission.

Would she finally get that taste of surrender she yearned for tonight?

Faith wanted tonight to be perfect. Which meant she had to look perfect. She drew her fingers through her hair. Earlier in the day, she'd dyed it a darker brown to compliment her look for the night. She'd felt the need to do something different with her hair. She usually changed it whenever she was feeling restless. And she was definitely feeling restless today, mostly in a good way.

She pulled a short leather skirt out of her closet along with a dark red blouse with a neckline in the shape of a deep V. The low cut meant Faith couldn't wear a bra with it, but that wasn't a disadvantage. She held it up before herself in the mirror. *Yes.* This was it. With some fishnet stockings, a pair of heels, and lipstick in her favorite shade of red, it would be the perfect outfit. One look at her, and Eve wouldn't be able to resist doing all those dirty things she'd threatened Faith with.

Faith hung the outfit up on the door of her closet, then sat down on her bed. She still had an hour before she had to start getting ready. Perhaps it was time to deal with the problem that had been plaguing her for weeks now. She still hadn't heard from her sister. Had something happened to her? Had Abigail's letters with Faith been discovered? There were so many possibilities, each worse than the last.

As much as she worried about her sister, there was a selfishness behind Faith's concerns. She didn't want to lose the one connection she still had to her past. Despite what she'd told Eve, Faith hadn't entirely let go of her old life. It was hard for her to admit it, but she longed for what she'd left behind, what she'd given up. Purpose. Meaning. Family. Love. It didn't make sense. Her family had turned their back on her. They'd shown her that their love had strings. And yet, Faith still missed them.

She grabbed her phone and dialed her aunt's number. Faith's aunt Hannah had taken her in after she'd left her family home at sixteen. Hannah had sympathized with her young niece, having done the same thing herself. At ten years older than Faith, Hannah had been something of a big sister to her. Faith had needed one at the time. After her sheltered upbringing, the real world had been a shock. Without Hannah, Faith would have been lost.

Hannah answered the phone. "Faith. It's so good to hear your voice. It's been a while."

"Hi, Hannah." Faith felt a pang of guilt. Since moving to the city for college, Faith and Hannah only saw each other once or twice a year. They used to speak on the phone at least once a week, but over time, Faith had gotten lazy when it came to keeping in touch. "Sorry I haven't called in so long."

"It's fine. How are you?"

"I'm good. I found a job."

Faith told Hannah about her new job, leaving out the part about her and Eve having a secret relationship. Although Hannah was nowhere near as conservative as the rest of their family, Faith doubted she'd approve, mostly because Eve was Faith's boss.

"Sounds like things are going well for you," Hannah said. "So you're staying out of trouble?"

Faith rolled her eyes. "I'm not sixteen anymore." Back

then, Faith had gotten into trouble constantly. She'd had a difficult time adjusting to her newfound freedom.

"How've you been?" Faith asked. "How are the kids?"

"They're great." Hannah filled Faith in on her life. Although she'd been single when Faith had lived with her, Hannah was married with kids now. Faith had no intention of ever getting married or living such a conventional life, but she envied the family Hannah had built for herself.

"So," Hannah said. "Is there a reason you called? I feel like you want to ask me something."

"That obvious, huh?" Faith said.

"I can tell there's something on your mind, that's all."

"You're right. It's my sister. I'm worried about her."

"The one you're still in touch with?" Hannah asked. "Abigail?"

"Yep. She writes to me every two months like clockwork, but her latest letter is overdue. I've written to her twice since then, and I've heard nothing back."

"You're worried something has happened to her?"

"Yeah," Faith said. "Or she got caught writing to me. That might be even worse. What if she's in trouble? And all because of me."

"It wouldn't be your fault, Faith. Your sister is an adult. She chose to keep in touch with you. Any trouble she gets in isn't your fault, or hers."

"I guess you're right."

"Look," Hannah said. "I'm still in touch with someone back home. A teacher at the high school. She's sympathetic to people like you and me. I'm sure she wouldn't mind finding out if anything has happened to your sister. Of course, if Abigail is fine, you won't know why the letters have stopped, but at least you'll know she's okay."

"That would be great, Hannah. Thanks for doing this."

"No problem," Hannah replied. "I'm always here if you need me."

They talked for a few more minutes until Hannah had to go. Faith hung up the phone, her gut churning with worry. There was one explanation for why her sister had stopped writing to her that Faith had refused to even consider until now. It was entirely possible that Abigail, like everyone else in her family, had started to believe that Faith's sin of betraying their religion was unforgivable. Maybe, like everyone else, Abigail had decided that Faith was dead to her.

It wouldn't surprise her. Her sister's letters had never been particularly warm or friendly. It was as if Abigail had been conflicted while writing them. They had this distant, factual tone, and they rarely contained any questions for Faith's life. Most of her letters were just superficial updates about their family. Her cousin had gotten engaged. Her oldest brother had a baby. The dogs had puppies. It wasn't much, but it was enough for Faith to know that her family was okay. And she still cared about them, despite everything. Despite the fact that they'd rejected her.

Faith had never really gotten over that rejection. She wanted so desperately to believe in people and the idea that love and acceptance were real. But it was hard to believe that when the people in her life who were supposed to love her unconditionally had turned their backs on her.

She pulled herself together. Now wasn't the time to dwell on the past. She had to get ready for tonight.

By the time Faith arrived at Lilith's Den, she was a jumble of nerves and excitement. She entered the foyer, where Eve had promised to wait for her, and scanned the room. It was 'ladies only' night again, and there were a few women milling about, but Faith couldn't find Eve.

Her eyes landed on a woman in a corset, with straight blonde hair and dark, smoky eyes. *Eve.* The corset she wore was different from the last time. This one was made of dark purple silk overlaid with black lace patterned with flowers. It was paired with a short black skirt, dark stockings, and those red-soled stiletto heels Faith had spotted in Eve's closet so long ago.

Faith's breath caught in her throat. For the first time, she felt like she was seeing Eve clearly. At first, she'd thought of Eve and the woman in the corset as two different people. As she and Eve had grown closer, and Eve had revealed more of herself, Faith had started to see Eve and the woman in the corset as two sides of the same coin. After all, Eve herself had said she thought of them as two different parts of her.

But that was wrong too. Eve and the woman in the corset were one. They were the same dominant, powerful, captivating woman who made Faith hunger for something she never thought she'd want. And Faith couldn't believe that this woman wanted her so badly that she was willing to risk everything.

Eve spotted Faith, her dark eyes lighting up. She beckoned Faith over. Faith's feet carried her to Eve's side.

Eve raked her eyes up Faith's body, her gaze brimming with lust. "You look so divine." She cupped Faith's cheek with her hand. "I'm going to enjoy showing you off tonight. Showing everyone you're mine."

Faith's pulse began to race. The idea of being possessed by anyone else would have unsettled her. But the idea of being possessed by Eve filled her with an undeniable heat.

"I have something for you," Eve said. "Something that will make sure every single person in this club knows that you belong to me."

Eve reached into her purse and produced a flat, square box. She opened it up and held it out to Faith, displaying its contents. Inside lay a wide choker-style necklace made up of rows and rows of sparkling diamonds.

Faith gasped. "Are those real?"

"Of course," Eve said.

Faith reached into the box and ran her fingers along the necklace. She'd never touched anything so precious. The choker wasn't the only thing in the box. Coiled beside the necklace was a chain as thick as a finger.

"The chain is platinum," Eve said. "Strong but beautiful. Only the best for my *pet*."

It all came together in Faith's mind. The necklace was a collar.

The chain was a leash.

Faith's skin began to tingle.

"I'll put it on for you." Eve took the choker out of the box. Brushing Faith's hair to the side, Eve fastened the collar around Faith's neck. It fit snugly. The silver felt cool against Faith's skin.

Eve stepped back, examining her. "It looks lovely on you. There's just one thing left to do."

Eve took the leash and clipped it to the small ring at the

front of the collar. She gave it an experimental tug. The delicate-looking chain was surprisingly strong.

"Don't worry, I won't make you crawl around." Eve slid her hand up the leash to the base of the collar, reeling Faith in closer. "At least, not this time."

Faith's mouth opened then closed again. Eve wasn't serious, was she?

Eve laughed softly. "Come on. Let's go inside."

Faith followed her to the door. She didn't have much of a choice with Eve holding the other end of the leash. Mercifully, the leash was long enough for them to walk a few feet apart.

They entered the club. Just like the last time Faith had visited Lilith's Den, it was packed with all kinds of women, all dressed richly, whether in leather, lace, or suits.

"Let's find somewhere to sit," Eve said. "Have a drink. Relax. Just the two of us."

"Sure." Faith glanced around. No one was giving Faith and Eve a second look. A woman being led around on a leash was completely normal here. Faith liked that. And she liked having this tangible symbol of the relationship between her and Eve. Faith belonged to Eve. She was Eve's treasured pet. There was no doubt about it.

Eve tugged on Faith's collar, pulling her toward the other end of the room. Faith was so distracted by everything around them that she almost tipped over as she hurried to follow. She was still just as in awe of the glamour and spectacle of it all as she'd been that first night in Lilith's Den. But this time she didn't feel any conflict or unease.

This time, it excited her.

They sat down in a dimly lit corner. A server came by to

take their drink orders. Eve draped an arm around Faith's shoulders, letting the leash hang loosely from her wrist. They lost themselves in each other's words, and touch, and the dark, kinky world of Lilith's Den.

Faith brought her hand up to the collar around her neck. She was starting to realize that what she felt for Eve was far more than just desire. Perhaps she was wrong to feel like she'd never again find that sense of belonging, that feeling like she had a place in the world. With Eve, she almost felt like she had that.

Eve reached out and drew her fingers through Faith's hair. "You look like you're enjoying yourself."

"I am," Faith replied. "Thanks for bringing me here tonight."

Eve smothered her with a kiss. Her lips were warm and soft.

Eve broke away. Her eyes wandered over to the far side of the room, where a crowd was gathered. There was a stage there, but Faith couldn't see it from their seat.

"Looks like there's a performance going on," Eve said. "Let's go take a closer look. I want you to see this."

Using the leash, Eve drew Faith up and led her toward the stage. They pushed through the crowd until they reached a spot from which they could both see clearly.

On stage were a pair of women. One was blindfolded and bound, her ankles tied together, her arms stretched up above her and tied to a hook hanging from the ceiling. She was on her tiptoes, dressed only in a bra and panties.

The other woman stood behind her, wearing leather from head to toe, a short whip with dozens of tails in her hand. Faith had seen one just like it in that drawer under

Eve's bed. Beside her was a table with several items on it. A feather. A lit candle. More whips.

From behind her, Eve wrapped her arms around Faith's body, pulling her in close. "Watch her," Eve said. "See the way her Domme mixes all the different sensations, pain and pleasure."

On stage, the woman kissed her submissive's neck tenderly while trailing the tails of the whip up the other woman's bare back. She whispered something into her submissive's ear, then drew back and struck the other woman's thighs with the whip, over and over.

The bound woman twitched and quaked, her muscles tense. But slowly her body slackened in its bonds, and her face took on a euphoric expression. It was like she was under the influence of some incredible drug. And each time the other woman struck her, she let out a pleasured cry that could be heard even over the club's music. Faith felt heat growing deep within her.

"Tell me." Eve's breath caressed Faith's ear. "What's going through your mind when you look at her? The submissive."

"How amazing that must feel," Faith said. "How much I want to feel what she feels."

On stage, the woman put down the whip and kissed her bound submissive with unexpected tenderness. Her submissive trembled at her touch. Was this that sweet surrender Faith had heard so much about? Was this what she craved?

"Eve?" Faith's voice shook. "Can you show me? Show me what that's like?"

"I can," Eve said softly. "I can show you here and now if you want."

Here and now? Faith looked around. The club was set up

with all kinds of equipment and restraints. No one was shy about using it all, but it hadn't occurred to Faith to try any of it out.

"Yes," she said. "I want that,"

"Even with everyone watching?"

Faith bit her lip in thought. There was something exhilarating about the idea, of having Eve toy with her while others looked on. Faith had never done anything like it before. But this was all new territory for her. And she wanted to explore it all.

She turned to face Eve. "Yes. Even with everyone watching."

Eve's lips twisted into a smile. "I knew from the day we met that you were the wild type. I underestimated just how wild you were." She wrapped the leash around her hand and gave it a tug, pulling Faith toward her. "Come with me."

CHAPTER SIXTEEN

Faith followed Eve away from the stage, the crowd thinning around them. They reached the back of the room where all kinds of equipment was set up. A big wooden cross. Something that looked like medieval stocks. A strange metal contraption that Faith couldn't even figure out how to use.

Eve wandered past it all, pulling Faith along behind her as she surveyed each piece of equipment. Faith's pulse thrummed in her ears. Had she really agreed to do this?

Eve waved her hand toward the cross. "All this is too showy." She stopped, her eyes fixing on the wall before her. "I prefer something simpler."

Faith followed the path of Eve's gaze. Bolted to the wall were four metal rings which formed the corners of a square. Two were near the ground and two were above head height. Attached to each ring was a short chain connected to a heavy metal cuff.

Something stirred deep in Faith's stomach. Cuffed

spread-eagled to the wall, Faith would be even more helpless than the woman on the stage. Eve would be free to do whatever she wanted with her.

"We're going to do something a little different," Eve said. "Red is still your safeword. But if you want me to slow down, say yellow."

Faith nodded, unable to break her eyes away from the wall.

Eve drew her in, letting her lips sweep against Faith's cheek. "You're safe in my hands, pet."

Eve kissed her gently. At once, Faith's nerves transformed into anxious excitement. Eve pulled her over to the wall and let go of the leash. One by one, she shackled Faith's wrists to the wall, locking each cuff with a small metal pin.

"Feet apart." Eve pressed her knee between Faith's thighs, pushing them apart. She dropped to her knees and cuffed both Faith's ankles.

Faith pulled at her restraints, testing them. The cuffs were lighter than they looked, but they were solid and strong. Faith's heart hammered against her chest. She was unable to move. Unable to free herself. Unable to do anything but let Eve toy with her. And the Eve who stood before her was different from the woman who had tied Faith up in her office. This Eve was far more intense and far less playful.

Eve unclipped the leash from Faith's collar and coiled it around her hand before placing it to the side. "I wasn't planning to do this with you here tonight. But I like the idea of showing everyone how complete your submission to me is."

Faith looked around. Though the club was full, almost

everyone was watching the stage or busy with their own play. But there were a few casual eyes on her and Eve, watching with mild interest. This was an everyday occurrence here. But for Faith, this was a first. The first time she let Eve fully take control over her. The first time she'd let anyone watch. And those watching eyes set her skin alight.

Eve drew her hand down the side of Faith's throat, her fingers brushing the collar. "It's a pity I didn't bring any of my toys," she said. "I'll have to improvise."

Eve waved over a wandering waitress and said something to her that Faith couldn't hear. The waitress disappeared. Faith didn't dare ask Eve what she was going to do with her. All she could do was squirm hopelessly in her chains.

Less than a minute later, the waitress returned. She placed a tray down on the table next to them. It held a single glass, filled to the brim with ice. Eve slipped the waitress a generous tip. Faith didn't know what Eve was playing at, but the waitress seemed unfazed by the unusual request.

Eve reached into the glass and pulled out two ice cubes. "Let's get started, pet."

Her eyes never leaving Faith's, Eve slipped one of the ice cubes between her lips. She leaned in and pressed her mouth to Faith's, the icy kiss sending a shock through Faith's body. It was so intense, so invigorating, that she almost forgot she was bound.

Something cool and hard slid down the side of Faith's neck. She gasped. It was the other ice cube. Her lips still on Faith's, Eve dragged the ice down the center of Faith's chest and between her breasts, leaving a trail of icy water behind.

Faith drew in a sharp breath. The sting of the ice felt good against her warm skin. She'd been overheated all night, a combination of the stuffiness of the club and the desire that Eve ignited in her.

Eve glided the ice cube all over Faith's chest, letting it linger on the parts of her breasts uncovered by her blouse. The cube of ice melted down to nothing, leaving rivulets running over Faith's numb skin. Eve took another ice cube from the glass and drew it over the curve of Faith's breasts, right next to the neckline of her blouse. Faith sucked air through her teeth. She was dangerously close to Faith's nipples. Was Eve going to expose her there and then?

Eve read her mind. "I'm a selfish Mistress," she said. "What's underneath those clothes is for my eyes only. And my hands."

She slipped the ice cube into the front of Faith's blouse and dragged it over her nipple. Faith hissed. The burning sensation was so intense that her knees threatened to give out from under her. The word 'yellow' formed in her mind. But as the shock passed, her whole body flooded with the most intoxicating sensation. And when the ice was replaced by Eve's soft, warm fingers, Faith almost collapsed.

"You see how good that feels?" Eve said. "The way pain and pleasure blend together?"

"Yes, Mistress." The words tumbled from her lips unbidden. She was losing control of her own mind as well as her body.

A smile played on Eve's lips. Inside Faith's blouse, Eve wore the ice cube down to nothing, then took another and teased Faith's other nipple with it. Faith shivered feverishly, overcome by all the conflicting sensations. All the while, the eyes of those nearby looked on, watching as Eve toyed with her bound, powerless submissive. And all the while, the fire in Faith's core grew hotter and fiercer.

Eve reached around and unzipped the back of Faith's skirt, just enough to slide her hand inside Faith's waistband. Eve slid the ice cube down into Faith's panties, letting it graze over her outer lips.

Faith jerked against the wall. The kiss of the ice, the frigid water dribbling into her slit, only inflamed her even more. She whimpered.

"I've heard that sound before." Eve pulled the ice cube up out of Faith's panties and tossed it aside. "You want me to fuck you, don't you?"

Faith's face grew hot. She hadn't intended this when she asked Eve to show her what it felt like to be the woman on stage. But everything about this was turning her on.

She nodded furiously.

"I don't know about that." Eve drew her hand further down, cupping Faith's mound. Her fingers still felt cool from the ice. "You belong to me alone. Your pleasure belongs to me alone. Why should I share that with anyone else? Why should I let anyone see that?"

Faith let out a soft whine, the need within her becoming unbearable. She pushed her hips toward Eve in vain. She could barely move in her bonds.

"On the other hand, I like showing everyone just how obedient a pet you are," Eve said. "Do you think they'd enjoy watching me make you come?"

"Yes," Faith said. "*Please.*"

"Please, what? Tell me what you want me to do to you."

Faith looked around. There were a few more eyes on the

two of them now. Although Faith was fully clothed, with Eve's hand down her skirt it was clear what was happening. But Faith wanted them to see. She wanted everyone to see how much Faith was Eve's, how masterfully Eve was able to command her body. She wanted everyone to know that Faith belonged to Eve completely.

She closed her eyes. "Please fuck me, Mistress."

At once, Eve slid her fingers into Faith's slit. There was no more teasing, no hesitation. Eve simply entered her with one shove. Faith shuddered, her eyes rolling into the back of her head. Something about being bound and teased for so long had set every nerve in Faith's body on edge.

Eve's ice-cooled fingers warmed inside her as they grew more frantic. Her lips crashed against Faith's again, her body pinning Faith against the wall. Faith writhed and tugged at her restraints. Eve's skin against hers, and her fingers inside, her warmth, her ravenous lips, her cool tongue, her taste—it was all too much.

Faith convulsed against Eve's body, straining against her chains as pleasure emanated out from her center, tearing through her like wildfire.

She gasped for air as she came back down from the pleasurable heights she'd reached, her body sagging in her bonds. Eve was right there with her, kissing her and holding her close.

"You're all right, pet." Eve stroked the back of her fingers down Faith's face. "I'm here. I'm going to release you now, okay?"

Faith nodded, her voice faltering.

"You did so well." Eve planted a gentle kiss on Faith's

cheek. "Once I get you out of these cuffs, I'm taking you somewhere I can have you all to myself."

Faith and Eve got out of the cab at the front of a hotel. The drive had cleared the haze in Faith's head, but it did nothing to stem the longing within her.

"I booked us a room for the night," Eve said. "I thought you might need to go somewhere quiet after Lilith's Den. Somewhere less intense."

Faith followed Eve inside. Eve had removed the leash, but the collar still adorned Faith's neck. Eve glanced around before getting into the elevator. She'd chosen a hotel across town, presumably so they wouldn't run into anyone they knew. Still, Eve didn't relax until they reached their room.

"There." Eve shut the door behind them. "We're finally alone."

Faith barely had a chance to admire the lavish suite before Eve was upon her, drawing her into an urgent kiss and sweeping her toward the bed.

They crashed upon it, a tangle of arms, lips, and lust. Faith deepened the kiss, letting her hands roam Eve's body, from her soft hair down to the swell of her hips. After being restrained, unable to touch, Faith needed to feel Eve, to taste her, to immerse herself in Eve's presence. Faith's desire hadn't been satiated by their performance in the club. What she wanted from Eve went deeper than any physical craving.

Eve got up and removed her heels, then slipped out of her skirt. Underneath, her thigh-high stockings were topped with lace and held up by a garter belt. Faith stared, unable to tear her eyes away. Eve seemed so much freer in the corset and garters than in anything else. So much more real.

So much more mesmerizing.

Eve leaned down, one knee on the bed, and drew Faith's blouse up over her head. Faith lay back down and lifted her hips, allowing Eve to pull her skirt from her legs, then her fishnet stockings, then her panties, until Faith lay there wearing nothing at all.

Eve's eyes rolled along Faith's body. The possessive look in them made Faith's heart skip a beat. Eve fell upon her once more, devouring her with her hands and lips, the touch of her tongue against Faith's feather-light. Faith dissolved into Eve, drinking in her taste, and her scent, and her very essence.

Eve skimmed her hand up the inside of Faith's thigh. Faith drew back slightly, feeling torn. It was clear that Eve wanted nothing more than to ravish her until she couldn't take it anymore. But that wasn't what Faith needed from Eve. She'd given Eve a part of herself that night, a part she'd never shared with anyone. She had so much more to give. But at the same time, she wanted a part of Eve.

Faith ran her hand down to where Eve's thighs met, drawing it over the lace of her panties. "Let me serve you, Eve. Let me please you.

Eve's breath shuddered. Without hesitation, she lay back against the pillows, drew Faith to her, and gave her a look that could only mean *yes*.

Gingerly, Faith peeled back Eve's panties, drawing them from her legs, then crawled back up to kiss her Mistress on her lips, savoring her sweet softness. She kissed her way down Eve's neck and chest to where her breasts peeked out the top of her corset. She pulled the corset down further, uncovering the perfect buds of Eve's breasts, kissing them until they pebbled under her lips.

One hand bracing herself on the mattress, Faith slipped her other hand between Eve's legs again, feeling her silky heat. She grazed a finger over Eve's swollen nub, eliciting a soft hum from Eve's chest.

"Go on," Eve said.

A shiver went through Faith's body. Eve's velvet voice always made her commands impossible not to follow. But tonight, there was a yearning in it that made Faith's heart flutter. And the way Eve trembled at her touch was so electrifying.

Eve parted her legs further, her hips rising toward Faith, urging her on. Slowly, Faith slid her fingers down to Eve's entrance, feeling the pulsing within her. She pushed two fingers inside, deeper and deeper, until she hit a spot that made Eve shudder.

"God, Faith." Eve's eyes fell closed. "Yes."

Faith sank her fingers inside Eve, over and over. Eve moaned and shook, grinding back into Faith. She slung her arm over Faith's shoulder, pulling her in until they were pressed together, the lace of Eve's corset rubbing against Faith's bare skin. The hotel bed quaked around them as their bodies rocked in tandem, so in sync that they moved as one.

Eve tensed against Faith as her pleasure rose, until, at last, Eve tipped her head back and let out a wild cry. Faith felt every tremor that went through Eve's body, felt Eve pulse around her fingers, felt Eve lose herself, until finally, her body stilled.

Faith crumpled onto the bed next to Eve. The other woman let out a long breath. Her eyes were closed, satisfaction written all over her face. There was something gratifying about seeing Eve this way, disarmed and uninhibited. Not wanting to break the silence, Faith curled up against her, an arm over the other woman's stomach.

After a while, Eve returned to her body. Idly, she drew her hand along the collar around Faith's neck, tracing the diamonds on it. Faith had forgotten she was wearing it.

"Tonight was really something," Eve said.

Faith murmured in agreement.

"I mean it. This was... different."

"Different how?" Faith asked.

Eve seemed to think for a moment. "I first started exploring all this a few years ago, after the separation. It became a release of sorts. But I've never done this with anyone I've felt so connected to. Not until you." She looked into Faith's eyes. "This is more intimate. More complete. More real."

"I... I feel it too." Faith had felt that connection, that pull, since the moment they'd met. It had only grown stronger since. "I've never done anything like this before, but it feels more intimate than anything else."

Eve gathered Faith in her arms and drew her in closer. Faith closed her eyes, sighing contentedly. She felt so light and free. Earlier, at Lilith's Den, she'd felt something close to that complete and utter surrender, but it had been just out of her grasp.

What would it take to reach that? She'd resolved the

conflict within her, embraced her submissive desires. But embracing everything she felt toward Eve? That was much harder. With so much standing in the way of Faith and Eve being together, she couldn't let herself believe this was real.

As long as everything between them had to remain a secret fantasy, she couldn't truly be Eve's.

CHAPTER SEVENTEEN

"Good morning," Eve said.

Faith entered the kitchen. "Hi."

She lingered by the doorway. She'd just arrived at work and the twins were still asleep. Eve herself looked like she'd just gotten out of bed. She was wrapped in a plush robe, her hair unbrushed and falling in loose, wavy curls. There was something endearing about seeing Eve in this wild state, at least compared to how she usually looked. She was still more put together than Faith was.

Eve held up her mug. "Would you like some coffee?"

"No thanks. I had some at home." Faith regretted it now. She wanted an excuse to stay here with Eve. "I'll go wake up the twins."

"Wait." Eve grabbed Faith's arm. "Don't. Not yet."

"I don't want them to be late."

"They won't be. And if they are, it's only one day." Eve pulled her close. "I want a few minutes alone with you."

"Okay." After all, Faith couldn't refuse Eve's commands.

Eve planted a soft, lust-filled kiss on Faith's lips before

breaking away. "I know we shouldn't do this," she said. "But I won't be able to make it through the morning otherwise. This is agonizing, having you around and not being able to touch you."

A knot formed in Faith's chest. She felt the same way. After that incredible night she and Eve had spent together, pretending that they were just a nanny and her boss was becoming unbearable.

"I'm getting so tired of all this sneaking around. If only I could take you out on a date." Eve's eyes sparked. "If I'm going to tie you up and have you do my bidding, the least I could do is buy you dinner first."

A smile tugged at the corners of Faith's lips. "If you were to take me on a date, where would we go?" It was pointless to even think about such things. The two of them weren't going to be able to go on a real date any time soon. But she couldn't help but indulge her imagination.

"Where to begin? There's an amazing Moroccan restaurant downtown. It's one of the city's hidden treasures. It's this whole incredible experience. They only seat ten people a night. I'd take you there first."

"And then?"

"Then, we'd go to a quiet little rooftop cocktail bar nearby and drink champagne and watch the city go by." Eve's voice fell lower than a whisper. "Then, I'd bring you back here, and I'd open up all those drawers under my bed one by one and spend the rest of the night torturing you with pleasure."

Warmth spread through Faith's body. "That sounds like the perfect night."

The light in Eve's eyes dimmed. "But that's all a distant

dream for now. This custody situation. Our relationship would complicate things."

"I know. It's okay. I understand."

Eve drew Faith to her again. "Whatever did I do to deserve you?"

She pressed her lips to Faith's once more. This time, the kiss drew out. Faith crumbled against the other woman's body, the scent and taste of Eve's coffee-tinged lips flooding her.

The sound of footsteps padding down the hall reached Faith's ears. Eve pulled away, groaning. Seconds later, Leah entered the kitchen, rubbing her eyes with her fists.

"Good morning, sweetie," Eve said.

She gave Leah an affectionate pat on the head. For all her sharp edges, Eve had a sweet, kind side. It showed at all the little moments she shared with Leah and Ethan.

"Why don't you go wake up your brother?" Eve said. "Breakfast will be ready soon."

Leah nodded sleepily and headed back out of the kitchen.

"She never wakes up by herself. God knows why she did today." Eve sighed. "I need to get ready for work. You should make sure Ethan wakes up."

"Okay," Faith said.

"I'll be in my room if you need me." Eve paused in the kitchen doorway. "How do you feel about me taking you back to Lilith's again?"

Faith's heart leaped. "I'd love that."

"Next week, then. When the twins are with Harrison." The softness in Eve's expression faded. "Don't forget, Leah's violin needs to be restrung. Drop it off in the afternoon. And Ethan has baseball practice."

Faith watched Eve disappear down the hall. So they were back to boss and employee.

It was going to be another long day.

That evening after work, Faith met Lindsey for dinner at a little Thai restaurant near her house. They sat down and ordered their food before getting into the important business of catching up. It seemed like an age since they'd last seen each other that weekend at Lindsey's house. So much had happened since then. So much had changed.

Faith had changed.

"So," Lindsey said. "How are things with Eve?"

"They're great," Faith replied. "Actually, we went back to Lilith's the other night. And we're going back again next week."

"Really?" Lindsey smirked. "And here I thought you weren't into 'that kind of thing.'"

"I wasn't. Not until her." Faith sighed. "There's just something about Eve that makes me want to be hers. She makes me feel things I've never felt before. She's brought out this whole new side of me."

"Maybe that side of you always existed. It just took someone special to bring it out."

"Maybe." Faith rested her chin on her hand. "Eve really is special. I have serious feelings for her."

"Have you told her that?"

"I don't want to make things harder than they already

are. This whole situation she's in with the kids, it's complicated."

Lindsey gave Faith a sympathetic smile. "I'm sure it'll all work out in the end."

"Yeah." But Faith was trying her hardest not to get her hopes up.

"And when it does work out, and you and Eve can stop hiding, we're going on a double-date. I haven't told Camilla about the two of you, but I'm pretty sure she's figured it out. Either that, or she's trying to set you and Eve up. She keeps hinting we should have both of you over for dinner."

Faith shook her head. "How are things with Camilla, anyway?"

"They're good. We're thinking of going away soon. Taking a trip around Europe. Camilla has some distant relatives in France that she hasn't seen in years."

As Lindsey filled her in, Faith's mind drifted back to the morning with Eve. She'd been walking on air since, daydreaming about the two of them going back to Lilith's Den. Although Faith still found going to Lilith's Den exciting, she mostly just wanted to go somewhere she and Eve could really be together.

Lindsey looked around. "Our food is taking forever. I'm going to the ladies room. Be right back." She stood up and headed to the restrooms.

Faith dug her phone out of her purse while she waited for Lindsey to return. She had a message from her aunt Hannah.

I have some news about your sister. Call me when you get the chance.

Finally! Faith hesitated. She just couldn't wait until after dinner. She had to know what was going on with Abigail.

She dialed Hannah's number. Hannah picked up after a few rings.

"I got your message," Faith said. "What have you heard?"

"There's good news, and there's bad news," Hannah said.

"Yes?" Faith waited with bated breath.

"I talked to that friend of mine, and she asked around. The good news is that your sister is fine. So is the rest of your family."

Faith felt a surge of relief. "What's the bad news?"

"I know why she hasn't sent you a letter in a while." Hannah hesitated. "I don't know the details, just bits of gossip my friend heard. Apparently, Abigail was caught talking with someone who left the church."

Faith's heart stopped. It could only be her.

"Her husband found out and got your parents and the church elders involved. It caused a big scandal, so word got around."

This wasn't good. Abigail would be facing serious repercussions for committing what was a major sin in her family's eyes.

And Faith would never get to speak with her again.

"Faith?" Hannah said. "Are you there?"

Faith cleared the lump in her throat. "Yes."

"I'm so sorry. I know how hard it is to go through this, especially a second time."

It was little consolation. At least Hannah had a family of her own now. But Faith had no one. Her last connection to her family, even though it had been tenuous, was gone now.

The only people in the world who were supposed to love her unconditionally had turned their backs on her.

Faith didn't blame her sister. She knew how hard it was to break free from a lifetime of brainwashing. Still, it stung. She should have seen it coming. She should have known Abigail would eventually get caught. Secrets don't stay secret forever.

Out the corner of her eye, Faith spotted Lindsey walking back to the table. "I should go. I'm at dinner. Thanks for looking into things for me."

"Are you going to be all right?" Hannah asked.

"Yeah, it's fine."

"If you need to talk, I'm here."

"I know. Thanks, Hannah." Faith hung up the phone.

Lindsey sat down. "Everything okay?"

"Yeah," Faith replied. "I was just talking to Hannah."

"Any news about your sister?"

"Not yet." Faith didn't like lying to Lindsey, but she didn't feel like talking about it.

"That's too bad. I'm sure you'll hear something soon. Hopefully good news."

Their dinner arrived and the conversation returned to Lindsey's travel plans with her girlfriend. Faith listened intently as she ate. She wasn't going to let everything with her sister upset her. In fact, this was a good thing. It meant Faith could finally leave her old life behind.

Right?

CHAPTER EIGHTEEN

*E*ve brushed Faith's hair over one shoulder and fastened the diamond collar around her neck. "No leash tonight," Eve said. "Think you can behave yourself without it?"

"I'll try my best," Faith replied.

They entered the crowded club. Eve drew Faith over to a quiet corner, hidden away from the rest of the club, and ordered them a bottle of champagne. Tonight, they weren't here to play. It wasn't one of the club's 'ladies only' nights. The last thing they wanted was to be fodder for the fantasies of gawking men. They were simply here to be with each other and immerse themselves in the atmosphere.

And yet, Faith felt none of the excitement she'd first felt when Eve first suggested they return to Lilith's Den. Being surrounded by all these people had Faith feeling empty. Ever since hearing the news about her sister she'd had this hollowness in her chest that wouldn't go away. All those feelings of rejection she'd thought she'd overcome years ago had come rushing back.

Faith refused to admit how much it upset her. She'd refused to let it show. She was good at that, at suppressing her feelings and pretending to be cheerful and happy. She'd spent most of her life pretending to be fine, when really, she'd felt trapped. She'd left that life behind long ago, but the way she was feeling now proved that she'd never truly escaped it.

As they waited for their drinks to arrive, Faith watched the club go by around her. Lilith's felt different this time. It had lost its luster. The whips, the chains, the excess—it all felt empty.

Faith pulled herself together. She wasn't going to let her feelings get in the way of enjoying herself with Eve. After all, wasn't that what mattered? That she was with Eve, and that they could be together freely?

Their drinks arrived. The champagne tasted flat.

Eve tucked a strand of Faith's hair behind her ear. "What's going on with you tonight?"

"Nothing." Faith plastered on a smile. "I'm not feeling this crowd, that's all."

"Neither am I." Eve leaned in closer. "How about we get out of here? Go somewhere I can have you all to myself?" Her lips brushed against Faith's cheek. "Or, if you're in the mood for something a little more interesting, there are private rooms upstairs that are well equipped with all kinds of naughty toys."

A shiver ran along Faith's skin. She couldn't deny how appealing that sounded. It would be a welcome distraction. But was that what she wanted right now?

Eve slipped a finger under Faith's collar, drawing her in for a hot, hard kiss. Faith melted into Eve's greedy lips. It was almost enough to make her forget about everything else.

"What do you say?" Eve asked. "I want to take you upstairs and do all kinds of wicked things to you."

Something twisted in Faith's gut. She wanted Eve, but not this. She shook her head, pulling away. "No."

"What's the matter?"

Faith didn't know how to answer her. She didn't know why everything suddenly felt so wrong. It was all just too much. She tugged at the diamond collar around her neck. It was too tight.

"Faith, what's going on?" Eve asked.

"I'm not your possession!" Faith crossed her arms between the two of them. "I'm not your pet. I'm not a thing. You don't own me."

Eve flinched. "I know that. Faith, I've never thought of you like that. I don't see you that way, I promise."

Faith's heart lurched. The hurt in Eve's eyes filled her with guilt. She wasn't mad at Eve. She was mad at herself. Everything was all messed up.

"I'm sorry." Eve reached out to touch Faith's arm, then pulled back. "I never meant to make you feel that way."

"I know. It's not you, I'm just—" Faith's voice quivered. "I can't do this right now. Be your submissive."

"Okay. That's fine. Let's just get out of here. Go somewhere just to talk."

"I just want to go home."

"At least let me take you." Eve held out her hand. "Please?"

Faith just wanted to be alone, but the softness in Eve's gaze swayed her. "Okay."

She slid her hand into Eve's, and Eve led her out of Lilith's Den.

The cab pulled up to Faith's apartment. Faith didn't get out of the car. She still didn't feel like talking, but she owed Eve an explanation for her behavior. She couldn't end the night with this hanging over them, especially since they might not have a chance to be alone again for a long time.

"Do you want me to come up with you?" Eve asked.

"Yeah," Faith said. "I'd like that."

They got out of the car, and Eve followed Faith up to her apartment.

"Come on in." Faith opened the door and turned on the light. She hadn't been expecting company. Fortunately, she'd tidied up in the morning.

Eve looked around Faith's living room. Her eyes fell on the old gray sofa. "This place is cozy."

Faith raised an eyebrow. For Eve, this was probably slumming it.

"I mean it. It reminds me of where I lived in college. I think I had the same couch." Eve sat down on it. "Come on. Sit. Let's talk."

Faith sat next to her. "I'm sorry about tonight."

"No, I'm sorry. I should have noticed you were feeling off."

"It's not your fault."

"It is," Eve said. "You're my submissive. You're new to all this. When emotions are running high, it's easy for things to go wrong. I need to be more vigilant."

"Still, it's on me to be responsible for my feelings," Faith said. "I guess I didn't realize I was so upset. Or maybe I just didn't want to admit I was upset."

Eve crossed her legs and shifted to face Faith. "What's been troubling you?"

"It's my little sister. We send each other letters. Well, we used to. I haven't heard from her for a while, and I just discovered why. She isn't supposed to be talking to me. No one in my family is. But she got caught, so she's stopped. She was my last connection to my family. Now I'm cut out from them entirely."

"Oh, Faith," Eve said. "I'm sorry."

"After everything I've been through with my family, this shouldn't upset me, but it does."

"What happened with them?" Eve asked. "Your family. You told me you left them because they wanted you to be something you're not?"

"Yeah. I mentioned that my family is religious. That's kind of an understatement. On the surface, the religion they follow seems like any other normal religion. But my family, the community they're part of, they take everything to extremes. There were all these rules and restrictions, most of them aimed at women. Men were the heads of everything. Women were expected to be nothing more than wives and mothers. There's a reason I'm good with kids. I'm the oldest of seven, so I grew up looking after all my siblings and cousins."

Faith folded her legs underneath herself on the couch. "The community, it was so insular. We were forbidden from associating with any nonbelievers on more than a superficial level. It was almost cult-like in that sense. And anyone who spoke out against the church? Or worse, anyone who left it? They were ostracized. Like my aunt Hannah. She left when I was nine. The way the adults all reacted to her leaving was so horrible. She just became this evil, toxic person to them. It was like she was less than human."

Faith's stomach knotted. Now Faith was that person to everyone in her family, even her sister. "I remember when Hannah disappeared. I asked my father what had happened to her. He grabbed my arms so hard and looked into my eyes with such raw hatred, and he told me never to ask about her again. Never to even speak her name again. It was the last time I ever brought it up. I had bruises on my arms for days."

Faith found Eve's hand on her arm. She'd been so lost in memory that she hadn't noticed how tense she'd gotten. It was comforting.

"But I never forgot about her, that aunt," Faith said. "And as I got older, I pieced together what happened to her, and I began to understand why she'd left. She was always a little eccentric. Different. That was why I liked her. I felt different too, growing up. No one else seemed to mind the constraints placed on them. Or if they did, they didn't show it. All the other girls seemed perfectly happy to one day get married, have kids, and live out their days serving their husbands, never leaving the town we grew up in.

"But that wasn't what I wanted for myself. I knew there was a whole world out there, beyond the confines of the cage that I lived in. I craved freedom. And things only got worse as I got older. My parents started talking about marrying me off as soon as I was old enough. They set up a meeting with one of our neighbors, a man who was ten years older than me, so we could start the courtship process. I was only sixteen."

"Sixteen?" Eve's face was marked with horror. "You were only a child. Your parents were going to force you to get married?"

"Not until I turned eighteen. And I don't know if they actually would have forced me to marry him. It was more like they simply expected me to do as they told me. I wasn't really a person, just property to be sold off, given away to a new owner like one of my family's puppies." Faith's stomach churned at the thought. "But I didn't want to get married. I was so confused about the idea. I had all these feelings, feelings I thought were wrong, for boys and for girls, and I didn't understand them. How was I supposed to? That kind of thing wasn't talked about. And we didn't even have a TV. All I knew were things I'd heard from kids from school, but none of it made sense. I just knew deep down that I'd never be able to figure myself out while living under the thumb of my family. I knew I had to get out.

"It wasn't as simple as that, of course. I had no money, nowhere to go. But I knew Hannah was out there somewhere. I started sneaking to the library to use the internet to track her down. It took a while, but I found her. We got in touch, and I told her about my situation. She was sympathetic, but I was a minor, so she couldn't do much. So I decided to take matters into my own hands." Faith's fists tightened in her lap. "I scraped together money for a bus ticket to the town Hannah lived in, and one day, instead of going to school, I got on the bus and left. I didn't leave a note in case my parents found it and tried to stop me. I planned to call them when I got to Hannah's house but the bus was delayed, so by the time I got there my parents had reported me to the police as missing. There was this huge search, and it was a big mess. I called my parents in the end, let them know I was safe, and where I was. They came to get me. But when I told them why I ran away, why I didn't want to go back with them, they just…"

Faith swallowed the lump in her throat.

"It was so stupid of me to think they'd react any way other than how they did," she said. "But I was their daughter. I thought it would be different with me. I prayed that they wouldn't be mad at me, but what happened was much worse. They didn't get angry at me. They didn't force me to go back with them or try to convince me to come home. They just left me there." Her voice cracked. "They gave up on me. To them, I was beyond saving. I was tainted. I could see it in the way they looked at me. I begged them not to cut me out of their lives. I told them I wanted to stay a part of the family. It was naive, but I still loved them. They were all I'd ever known. But they refused. They cut me off. I was dead to them."

"I can't imagine how awful that must have been," Eve said. "No one should ever have to go through that, especially as a teenager."

"It was hard, but I was lucky enough to have Hannah to help me through everything," Faith said. "I tried my best to move on, to start a new life. But I still missed my old life. My home. My family. That longing, it never really went away. Then one day, when I was in college, I got a message from my sister Abigail on social media. She'd made a profile just to find me and talk to me. She wanted to reconnect, but she didn't have a computer she could use without anyone getting suspicious, so we decided to send letters instead. She was married by then, and stayed home while her husband worked, so she was the one who got the mail. She could easily hide my letters. We came up with an arrangement. Abigail would send me a letter at the end of the month, and I'd write back to her next month, and so on. Any more often than that would be too risky. We took all these precautions, but in the end, she got caught. And now, my only connection to my family is gone."

Faith sighed. "I was the one who chose to leave. I should be happy that I'm free to live my life the way I want. And I am happy, most of the time. But sometimes, I miss that life. I miss my family. I shouldn't want their love. They rejected me. Why do I still care about them?"

"Oh, Faith," Eve said. "You're only human. It's not wrong to want all that. Love, family, a place to belong. And it's not wrong to be disappointed when people let you down, especially when those people are family. You can't be expected to stop caring about them despite everything."

"But they don't care about *me*. They're supposed to, aren't they? That's what family does."

"You're right. That's what family is supposed to do. But sometimes family lets you down. Sometimes, you have to find your own family in the people who make you feel like you have a place in the world." Eve put her hand on Faith's. "I know this probably doesn't help right now, but you're not alone, Faith. You have people who care about you. You have friends. You have your aunt."

Faith felt a pang of guilt. For all her talk of having no family, she'd forgotten all about Hannah, and Lindsey, and everyone who had acted as her family the past few years.

Eve squeezed Faith's hand. "And you have me."

"Thanks," Faith said. "It really means a lot."

Eve wrapped her arm around Faith's shoulders. "I know that no one can replace your family, but I'll be here for you all the same."

Faith felt a surge of warmth. Eve was right. Faith wasn't alone in the world. She had people who loved her.

But life had taught her that love always came with conditions.

CHAPTER NINETEEN

When Faith arrived at Eve's house, the sun was setting. She unlocked the front door and headed inside. The twins were due back from their father's that evening, and Eve had asked Faith to come by to help prepare them for the week ahead.

Faith walked down the hall, searching for Eve and the twins. The house was far too quiet. "Eve?" she called.

She heard a clatter in the kitchen. A moment later, Eve came out into the hall, drying her hands with a dish towel. She wore an elegant blue dress that made her hazel eyes look greener, especially without her glasses. She was dressed much too nicely for a night in with the twins.

"Eve. Wow." Faith stared. "Are you going somewhere?"

"Not exactly," Eve said. "I need a minute. Why don't you wait for me in the lounge room?"

"Are the twins back? Is there anything you need me to do?"

Eve put her hands on her hips. "What I *need* is for you to go wait in the lounge room."

Faith frowned. "Okay."

She went into the lounge room and sat down. Eve was behaving strangely. What was going on?

After a few minutes that seemed to stretch out forever, Eve appeared.

"Is everything okay?" Faith asked. "Where are the twins?"

"At their father's." Eve sat down next to her. "I asked him to keep them for one more night. I don't like asking Harrison for favors, but this is important."

"What's going on?" Faith was starting to worry.

Eve folded her hands in her lap. "I've been thinking about the other night. About you and me. About us. It made me realize something. You need more from me than what I've been giving you. More than to be my *possession*."

She held up her hand, cutting off Faith's protest. "There was truth to what you said. I've gotten so carried away with this game we've been playing, and it's made me careless. I need you to know that you're more to me than a plaything. I want to show you that when I say you're mine, it goes so much deeper than anything physical. I want you to feel just how much you mean to me. So tonight, I'm going to show that. I can't take you out on a date, but I'm going to give you the closest thing. We're going to have dinner together. Just the two of us, here." Her voice dropped low. "And after dinner, I'm going to show you the height of intimacy that comes with complete surrender."

"Eve." Faith's stomach fluttered. "That sounds perfect."

Eve clasped her hands together. "Now, I just finished making dinner. Why don't you have a seat in the dining room and I'll bring it out?"

Faith practically floated into the dining room, Eve's

words playing in her mind, and sat down at the table. It was already set, not with the dinnerware they used every day, but with fine china, sparkling silver cutlery, and intricately folded white napkins. An arrangement of flowers sat in the center of the table.

Eve entered the room carrying two plates and set them down on the table. "I have a white that will pair well with this. I'll grab a bottle."

Faith stood up. "I'll get the glasses."

Eve gave her a sharp look. "Sit down. Tonight, you don't work for me."

Faith did as she was told. She stared at the dish before her while she waited for Eve to return. Arranged artfully on the plate was a tantalizing salmon dish that wouldn't have looked out of place at an expensive restaurant. It must have taken Eve hours to prepare. The idea of Eve slaving away in a kitchen was so at odds with the image Faith had of her.

It was funny how, over time, that image had changed. The prim and proper woman Faith had met on the day of the job interview had been replaced by the woman who wore corsets and took pleasure in chaining Faith to the wall.

Eve returned with the wine and poured them each a glass, then sat down across from Faith. "Dinner is served."

Faith took a bite of her salmon. It tasted as good as it looked. "This is incredible."

"It's an old family recipe, along with the salad," Eve said. "But dessert is my own creation."

Faith swallowed another mouthful. "What's for dessert?"

"The most decadent chocolate cream pie you've ever tasted. But we're going to save it for later. For afterward."

"After what?"

Eve sat back and narrowed her eyes at Faith. "You're full of questions this evening, aren't you? You'll have to wait and see. Right now, your only job is to relax and eat your dinner."

"You're the boss." A smile tugged at Faith's lips. "Thanks for all this. With everything that's been going on, I really needed it."

Eve's expression softened. "How've you been doing?"

"I'm okay. Honestly, more than anything else, I was upset with myself for being so upset. For not being able to let go of that old life. But maybe I don't have to let go of it altogether. There was some good stuff with the bad, after all. It was nice, being part of a big family. And there was this automatic sense of community, of belonging. Everyone was generous and kind." Faith sighed. "That was, as long as you did what was expected of you."

"It sounds like a lot of pressure," Eve said.

"It was. I was never very good at following the rules. There were just so many. Women weren't even allowed to wear pants or cut their hair. I can't even imagine what my life would have been like if I hadn't left. I guess I'd be just like my little sister. Married with three kids, living a life of domesticity. Not that there's anything wrong with that," Faith added.

"Believe me, I'm with you there. I was never suited for that life either."

"I'm just glad I have a choice now. That I have control over my own fate." Faith took a long sip of her wine. Freedom sure tasted sweet.

As dinner wore on, evening turned to night, and Faith

found herself opening up more and more about her old life. She didn't usually talk about it much. Everything about her upbringing was so alien to most people. But Eve seemed to understand her in a way no one else did.

"It must have been difficult, leaving it all behind," Eve said. "Giving up everything you knew. Adjusting to a new life."

Faith nodded. "It was a big culture shock. I had to learn everything I thought I knew about the world all over again. It was hard, but not as hard as it could have been. Up until that point, for my life, I felt like the world I lived in didn't make sense. It was only after I left home that I was finally able to understand myself. Don't get me wrong, there was a long adjustment period. It took me months not to feel weird wearing jeans. And when I finally realized how much freedom I had, I went a little wild."

She thought back to her high school and college days. They'd been filled with drinking, partying, and fooling around. "But all that experimentation and exploration helped me figure a lot out. About myself, about my sexuality. And when I did figure it all out, I didn't have any negative feelings. It was a relief. It was like this whole world had opened up for me, one where I could be whatever I wanted to be, and love who I wanted to love, and experience all these things I never dreamed of. I eventually settled down, but there's still plenty I haven't figured out about myself."

"I've been thinking about it, and you're right," Eve said. "Life is just a constant quest to find ourselves. I've been doing a lot of that over the past few years too."

"I guess your world must have changed pretty drastically when you got divorced," Faith said.

"It did, and in a good way. It forced me to find out who I really was. I had to wrap my head around my attraction to women too. It was always something I suspected about myself, but I never got to explore it until the separation." Eve's lips curved up slightly, her eyes fixing on Faith's. "Since then, I've learned far more about myself and my tastes beyond just liking women."

"You mean, like how much you like having women tied up on your bed, so to speak?" Eve had mentioned her first foray into the world of BDSM had been after her separation.

"Exactly. But you should know, although there were women before you, you're the only one I've had bound up in my bed."

Faith bit back a smile. "Didn't you promise that you'd tie me up on your bed in person sometime?"

"I did. And I have every intention of keeping that promise." Eve picked up her glass of wine. "Just as soon as we finish dinner."

CHAPTER TWENTY

After dinner, Eve led Faith to her bedroom. Once they were inside, Eve went over to the dresser and retrieved a small, familiar key. It was the key to the drawers underneath her bed.

Faith waited in silence, anxiety swirling within her. From the moment she'd laid eyes on Eve at Lilith's Den all those nights ago, all she'd wanted was Eve to show her the depths of surrender. But now that she was faced with it, she felt wholly unprepared.

Eve unlocked a drawer and pulled it open. Inside was a selection of ropes in different colors and sizes, all neatly coiled, along with several pairs of handcuffs and restraints made of leather.

Eve withdrew two lengths of thick white rope and placed them on the bed. Wordlessly, she beckoned Faith to her. Piece by piece, she stripped off Faith's clothes. The soft brush of Eve's fingers made goosebumps sprout on her skin.

Eve unclipped Faith's bra and slid it from her shoulders, leaving her in just her panties. She raked her eyes down

Faith's body. Faith resisted the impulse to shield herself with her arms. Something about the way Eve looked at her made her feel even more exposed than she was.

Without taking her eyes off Faith, Eve pulled off her dress, letting it fall to the floor, and removed her bra and panties. Faith drank Eve in with her eyes. It was the first time she'd seen Eve naked, and it was a sight to behold. The other night, Faith had thought there was nothing more irresistibly dominant than Eve in just a corset. She'd been so wrong. Here and now, before Eve's bare body, Faith was gripped with an urge to fall to her knees and to worship every part of Eve like she had the other night.

Instead, she stood by, her head bowed, awaiting Eve's command.

"Lie down on the bed for me," Eve said.

Faith climbed onto the bed and lay down. All the covers and cushions had been removed, leaving only a single pillow and dark silk sheets that felt smooth against her bare skin. The ropes lay on the bed next to her.

Eve joined Faith on the bed, straddling her body. Eve's weight atop her felt overpowering. But it was the sight of Eve, looking down at Faith with her breasts bared and her eyes ablaze, that took Faith's breath away.

Eve drew Faith's arms up toward the headboard, then picked up one of the coils of rope. She unwound it carefully. "Remember your safewords. Red. Yellow."

Faith nodded. Eve brought Faith's wrists together and looped the rope around and through them before tying a finishing knot. She took the tail of rope and pulled Faith's arms up, tying her wrists to the headboard.

Faith looked up. Her arms were stretched high above

her. She wriggled her arms. The knots binding her wrists were strong and secure.

"Stop that." Eve looked down at Faith, her gaze hard. "Faith, what I need from you right now is for you to let go. To let all resistance fall away. To trust me. Can you do that for me?"

"Yes." In truth, Faith didn't know if she could give Eve what she demanded, but she wanted to with all her heart.

Still straddling Faith's body, Eve picked up the other coil of rope and turned herself around so she was sitting atop Faith's thighs, facing away from her. Faith stared at the other woman's smooth, hourglass-shaped back as she took Faith's ankles and bound them together.

Eve got up from her perch on Faith's thighs and looked down at her hungrily. With her wrists and ankles bound together, her body stretched out, Faith could barely move at all. She couldn't help but feel like she was a dish on a platter, served up for Eve.

Eve slid her hands down Faith's sides. "You look so lovely, laid out for me like that." She grabbed the waistband of Faith's panties and drew them all the way down to her bound ankles.

Faith let out a shuddering breath. She'd been tied up by Eve before, but not like this. Not naked and helpless, all alone with her. But Faith wasn't powerless. She had her words. *Red. Yellow.* She could control what happened next. She could choose to make everything stop. She could choose to take it slow.

Or, she could choose surrender.

Faith closed her eyes and let calm wash over her. It did nothing to still her racing heart. But her heart wasn't racing out of fear. Every part of her body was screaming for this.

Cradling Faith's cheek in her hand, Eve dipped down to speak into her ear. "That's it. Just relax. Give in to all those wonderful feelings."

Eve kissed her, long and slow. Faith dissolved into Eve's lips. Gently, Eve rolled Faith onto her stomach then got up from the bed. The bed shook beneath Faith as Eve opened and closed a drawer underneath it.

A moment later, Faith felt something soft and flat skimming across her back. She opened her eyes and twisted around to look. Eve stood by the bed, a long, thin riding crop in her hand. She drew it up the side of Faith's neck. A shiver went through her.

"Keep your eyes closed," Eve said.

Faith obeyed.

"Remember what we spoke about the other night? About mixing pain and pleasure?" Eve swept the riding crop down the curve of Faith's back, over her hipbones to the flesh of her ass cheeks. "I'm going to show you how a little pain makes the pleasure so much sweeter."

Silence fell over the room. Despite everything, all Faith felt was calm. When Eve began tapping Faith's ass cheek with the riding crop, that feeling only intensified. Each smack made Faith tingle all over. She pressed her cheek into the pillow, sinking into the bed as Eve slapped her harder and harder. The skin on her cheeks grew warm.

Suddenly, Faith felt a sharp sting on her ass, accompanied by a loud crack. She hissed. It should have shocked her out of her trance-like state. But as the heat dissipated through her, she found herself falling even deeper.

Eve ran the flat of the crop along Faith's ass cheek. "More?"

"Yes," Faith murmured. "Please."

Eve continued to strike her with the crop, one cheek after the other, the leather tip biting into her skin. Her whole body began to burn, her core flaring hot and bright, her veins flooding with adrenaline and desire.

She didn't know how long she lay there for, thrashing and squirming as Eve assailed her with the riding crop, loud cracks echoing through the room. The next thing she was aware of was a cooling hand on her ass. She peered over her shoulder, straining against the ropes binding her. Eve kneeled next to her, caressing her freshly spanked ass cheeks.

Faith lay back down with a sigh. Eve's touch felt exquisite. As the pain faded, she felt the warmth from her cheeks spreading deep into her. Eve's touch on her sensitized skin went from soothing to electrifying, sending sparks slithering between her lower lips. The fact that her legs were tied together only intensified the heat between them.

Faith ground against the bed, trying to put out the fire within. She let out a whimper.

Eve slid her hand down, forcing it between Faith's bound thighs, her fingers pushing into Faith's slit. "Do you see now? All that pain has primed your body for pleasure. And how I love seeing you so ready and eager." She drew her hand back up, tracing a wet finger over Faith's ass cheek. "Had enough of pain? Ready for some pleasure?"

"Yes," Faith whispered. She arched her back, urging Eve's fingers into where she wanted them.

Eve turned Faith onto her back and began untying her ankles. They were already trying to break free. Once her bonds were undone, Eve pulled Faith's panties from where they were tangled around her ankles, tossing them behind her, and pushed Faith's legs apart.

Anticipation flared inside her. Eve clawed her way up Faith's thighs, coming to rest with her head between them. Faith strained toward her, anticipation flaring inside. With her wrists still bound to the headboard, she couldn't move far.

"Eve," she whined.

Eve grabbed onto Faith's waist and drew her fingernails down Faith's sides, leaving long pink scratches behind. Still, she didn't give Faith what she so clearly wanted. Faith writhed and twisted about, but it was futile. Defeated, she settled back against the bed, lying still.

After what felt like an eternity, Eve parted Faith's lips with her tongue and ran it up Faith's slit. Faith shuddered. The way Eve swirled her tongue over Faith's folds and probed at her swollen nub set her whole body alight.

Faith bucked and writhed, overcome. Her ass still stung, a ghost of the earlier pain, but it was like the spanking had charged her body. Now, after only minutes, she was ready to explode.

"Eve. Oh, Eve—"

Faith cried out, ecstasy surging through her. Her muscles tightened, her thighs clenching around Eve's head and her arms pulling at the ropes. Eve continued, milking every last drop of pleasure from her until her body went slack, unable to take any more.

Faith let her head fall to the side. The silk pillow was

cool against her warm cheek. Distantly, she felt Eve's hands at her wrists, untying the ropes that bound them. She was barely aware of her body, having been reduced to a puddle of lust.

Eve drew Faith's arms back down, pulling her close and kissing her. A soft murmur escaped her. Although Eve's kisses were gentle, there was a need in them, a possessiveness mixed with desire. Faith's hands drifted lazily down Eve's body, feeling her curves. Eve quivered at her touch.

"Faith." She cupped Faith's cheeks in her hands. "Do you want to please me?"

"Yes," Faith replied. "Always."

Eve lay her hands on Faith's shoulders, pushing them downward in a wordless command. Faith crawled down Eve's body, exploring every part of her Mistress with her lips. Her neck, which smelled of perfume mixed with Eve's natural scent. Her collarbone, her shoulders, her breasts, round and full. Those delightful pink nipples that pebbled between her lips and under her tongue. Her stomach, soft and smooth, her hips and thighs. That soft hair between them.

Eve shifted against her, her hips pushing out. Faith drew her lips up to where Eve's thighs met and slid her tongue into Eve's slit. She snaked it up and down, relishing the sweetness of Eve's arousal, letting Eve's scent flood her. A purr rumbled through Eve's body, her hand falling to Faith's head. She threaded her fingers through Faith's hair, pulling her in harder.

Faith worked her mouth between Eve's legs, her tongue flickering and lips sucking. Eve let out a fevered moan, her hips rising up into Faith. Faith hooked her arms under Eve's thighs. Eve's legs settled on her shoulders.

"Yes," Eve said. "Worship me."

Faith worshiped the goddess before her with wild abandon. Faith needed to please her, to serve her, to take her to the same heights of pleasure Eve had brought her to. She lost herself, drunk on Eve, consumed by her. She was Eve's, body, mind, and soul.

This was the surrender she craved.

She felt the pressure building within Eve's body.

"Oh yes," Eve said. "Oh, Faith!"

A heartbeat later, Eve shattered around her, her cries of surrender filling the room. Faith didn't stop until Eve edged away, overcome.

They fell back down to the bed together, their bodies wrapped around each other. Faith could feel the rise and fall of Eve's chest against her own. Eve pressed her lips against Faith's with a tenderness that was so unlike the woman who had been raining blows down on her with a riding crop just minutes ago. Or had it been hours? Faith didn't know. She didn't care. All that mattered was Eve. Faith just wanted to drown in her skin.

But this delightful dream of theirs had to end. Slowly, the rest of the world came crawling back, reality setting in.

Faith's eyelids fluttered open. Eve was beside her, gazing back into her eyes.

"Welcome back to the land of the living," she said.

"What time is it?" Faith murmured. It had to be getting late. She couldn't stay here in Eve's bed forever. They'd broken so many rules tonight, crossed so many of the boundaries they'd set.

"Why? Do you have somewhere to be?"

Faith sat up slowly. "No, but—"

Eve pressed a finger to Faith's lips. "We have the house to ourselves until tomorrow evening. No one knows you're here. I wasn't planning on letting you leave this bed until at least midday."

Faith yawned and lay back down. "If you say so."

"And I'm not done with you yet. There's one more thing I want to do with you." Eve kissed Faith on the forehead and got up. "Stay right there."

As Eve left the room, Faith sprawled out across the bed. She wasn't going anywhere. She was so deep under Eve's spell that she was powerless to do anything but obey.

CHAPTER TWENTY-ONE

When Eve returned a minute later, she was carrying two bowls heaped with freshly whipped cream.

Faith sat up and dragged her fingers through her hair. "Is that dessert?"

"Chocolate cream pie, as promised." Eve handed her a bowl.

Suddenly, Faith was ravenous. She took a bite. It was sweet, rich, and tasted homemade in the best way. "Mm. This is just what I need right now."

"This is why I saved dessert." Eve slipped into bed next to her, her own bowl in her hand, and stretched her legs out. "Sweet things and aftercare go well together."

"What's aftercare?" Faith asked between mouthfuls.

"You're feeling really good right now, aren't you? Light. High."

Faith nodded.

"Eventually, you're going to come down from that high. Aftercare is a dominant's way of catching you when you do.

It's me keeping all the good feelings flowing so you don't crash." Eve gestured toward the ropes still dangling from the headboard. "All this can be intense. Overwhelming. It can leave a person feeling vulnerable and raw, mentally and emotionally."

"I don't feel like that."

"Maybe not right now. But you still need this." Eve took a bite of pie and placed her bowl on the nightstand next to her. "Besides, this is as much for me as it is for you. I'll let you in on a little secret. It's not just the submissive that surrenders to her dominant. A Domme must surrender to her true desires, the kind that society considers perverse and twisted. She must trust her submissive to accept that dark side of her. It's a vulnerable state to be in."

"I never thought about it that way," Faith said. "This is all so much more complicated than I thought." She looked at Eve. "How did you get into this? Being a Domme, I mean?"

"Do you want the short answer or the long answer?"

"The long one." This was a big part of who Eve was. Faith wanted to know why.

Eve reached toward the foot of the bed and picked up the rope she'd used to bind Faith's ankles. "There was more to my marriage and divorce than I told you. More to what happened between me and Harrison and the rest of his family." She drew the rope through her hands, straightening out the kinks, then began tying it in a knot. "His parents, they were constantly trying to control our lives. Pressuring me to have children, to quit my job. At first, Harrison would stand up to them, but over time, he began to side with them. And when I became pregnant with the twins, it all became so much worse."

Eve finished her knot, then started on another one. "I ended up in the hospital because of complications from the pregnancy. I was drained of all my strength—physically, mentally, emotionally. I wasn't myself. And when I almost lost the twins, I was so afraid. I was vulnerable and weak, and Harrison, he took advantage of that to convince me to finally quit my job. He told me that I had to do what was best for the twins. That I was being selfish by continuing to work. That by putting my desires first, I'd be failing my children. There's so much pressure, as a mother, to make the right choices, and his words, they just ate at me."

This wasn't the first time Eve had spoken of Harrison's manipulative tendencies, but Faith hadn't expected anything so extreme. How could anyone be so cruel toward someone they were supposed to love?

"His mother was even worse." Eve began tying another knot in the rope, this time looping it over and under in a complex pattern. "We were never close until I became pregnant, then suddenly, I was her beloved daughter. My parents had moved to England by then, and my mother was dealing with some serious health issues, so they weren't able to visit. Eleanor stepped into my mother's role, staying by my bedside while I was in the hospital. She pretended to be sympathetic, while really she was manipulating me. She convinced me that I'd be a bad mother if I didn't fully dedicate myself to the twins. This was while there was still a chance that I'd lose them. I spent the rest of my pregnancy in the hospital, terrified that the twins wouldn't make it. So when they were born happy and healthy, I was so relieved."

Eve looped the rope once more and pulled it tight, leaving an elaborate knot in the middle. "But still, I was unhappy. I loved the twins so much, but I just felt empty. As time went on, as they grew up, those feelings didn't go away. I needed something more to be fulfilled. Eventually, I decided something had to change. I told Harrison I was going back to work, but he forbade it. By then, I was so worn down from constantly being controlled by him and his family that I didn't fight him. And I was too depressed to see how messed up my situation was. Instead, I just became even more withdrawn. Harrison couldn't understand why I was so unhappy. I had the perfect life. I had everything a woman could possibly want. His mother told me the same thing. That my family should be enough for me."

Eve stared down at the knotted rope in her hands, guilt written all over her face. "I started to feel like there was something wrong with me. I started to believe that I was a bad mother. Eleanor certainly didn't help dispel that idea. She was so critical of everything I did. And she stopped me getting help for the way I was feeling. She threatened me, said that if I went to the doctor or spoke to anyone about my problems, she'd have me declared mentally unfit and have the twins taken away from me. She didn't have any real basis for it, of course. But at the time, I believed her."

Anger erupted deep inside Faith. Just the idea of someone trying to tear the twins from Eve filled her with rage.

"It was my own mother who saved me," Eve said. "My parents, they came to visit for the first time since the twins were born. As soon as my mother saw me, she knew something was seriously wrong. I ended up breaking down in her arms, sobbing, telling her everything. She was horrified by how bad things had gotten. She helped me see how toxic

Harrison and his family's influence was and convinced me to seek help for my depression. She encouraged me to try a separation and helped me realize I could escape the life I was trapped in. When I started the divorce process, it was a weight off my shoulders. I knew it was the right decision. But still, I felt so hopeless. So powerless. I was lucky to have supportive and loving friends and family, but I'd been helpless for so long that I didn't know how to feel otherwise. Then one day, I crossed paths with an old friend of mine."

Eve pulled at one end of the rope. The last knot she'd tied vanished completely. "Her name is Vicki. We met in business school but fell out of touch because our lives went in vastly different directions. I got married and started a family, while she was living the life of a womanizing party girl. We ended up reconnecting, and when I told her about the separation, she made it her mission to help me make the most of my newfound freedom. She dragged me out to bars and parties, encouraged me to explore my sexuality. It was her way of being supportive. And it helped. I'd been living this restrictive, conventional life for so long, I'd forgotten how to have fun." She ran the rope through her hands, feeling each knot. "One day, Vicki invited me to go to Lilith's Den with her. She'd always been open about her tastes, but I'd never shown an interest in anything like that. I went along with her anyway. That night, it changed my life."

Faith thought back to the first time she'd gone to Lilith's Den. She'd felt the same way. Just walking through the door had awakened something in her.

"There was something so empowering about it," Eve continued. "Seeing all those strong, self-assured women who were completely in control. And the submissives. There was this power in them too, in vulnerability so freely given. It opened my eyes to a world where women could explore their sexuality, let out their true selves, discover their inner strength. I think that's why Vicki took me there. She must have sensed that it was something I needed. She was right. Lilith's Den helped me crawl out of the hole I was in, helped me take back control. It helped me rebuild my life and gave me the confidence to pursue what I wanted. It helped me live again.

"It's been a few years since then, and this?" Eve held up the rope. "It still makes me feel the way it did that very first night at Lilith's Den. And lately, those feelings have only gotten stronger." Her eyes met Faith's. "With you, those feelings have only gotten stronger."

Faith's heart sped up.

"That part of me," Eve said. "That woman in the corset. Until now, I've never let her be anything more than a persona. But being with you has made me realize she's as much a part of me as any other. Being with you makes me feel more complete and more alive than I have in years."

"Eve," Faith said softly. "I feel that too." She'd never felt freer than when Eve had her bound up in ropes. She'd never felt more content than when Eve had her arms around her. She'd never felt happier than when Eve said Faith was hers.

Eve tossed the rope aside and pulled Faith down to the bed, drawing her into an embrace. "As soon as we're free to be together, I'm going to treat you how you deserve to be treated. I'm going to take you out, and spoil you, and show the world you're mine. There are many more nights like this ahead."

"I can't wait." Faith melted into Eve's arms. She was starting to come down from that high, but with Eve by her side, it was impossible to feel anything but serene.

But at the back of her mind, Faith was still wary. It was too early to start dreaming about the future.

Too much was still up in the air.

CHAPTER TWENTY-TWO

It was nighttime when Faith received a phone call from Eve.

Faith was lounging around at home on one of her days off after having worked seven days in a row. That week had seemed tortuously long. Being around Eve, while keeping things strictly professional, was harder now than ever. And yet, being apart from Eve was even worse.

Faith had fallen hard.

She picked up the phone, eager to hear Eve's voice.

"I need you to come to the house," Eve said. "Now."

"Sure." Faith frowned. Eve's voice had a hard edge. "Is everything okay? Is it the twins?" They were supposed to be at their father's.

"I'll explain when you get here."

"I have to get dressed first, then I'll be right over."

"Just make it quick." Eve hung up the phone.

Dread rolled down Faith's back. Something was very wrong. She could hear it in Eve's voice.

She threw on some jeans and a jacket, grabbed her keys,

and headed to Eve's house. It was late, and there was no traffic, so it wasn't long before she arrived.

She unlocked the door and let herself in. The house was eerily silent. "Eve?"

"In here," Eve called.

Faith followed Eve's voice to her office. Inside, Eve stood by her desk, her back to the door.

"Eve?" Faith said quietly. "Are you okay?"

Eve turned. Her face was deathly pale, and her lips were pressed into a thin line. She was staring down at the phone in her hand.

Faith approached her. "What's going on?"

"It's Harrison. He—" Eve swallowed. "It's easier if I just show you."

Eve handed her phone to Faith. A video was queued up on the screen, but it was too dark to see anything. Faith pressed play. The video looked like it had been taken inside a bar or club. As it played on, the crowd came into focus. Most of the people were dressed in skimpy, provocative clothing. In the background, all kinds of unusual fixtures and equipment could be seen.

Instantly, Faith knew where the video had been taken. "This is Lilith's Den."

Eve didn't respond. She didn't need to.

The video zoomed in on some seating in a corner, hidden away from the main floor of the club. Despite the dim lighting, the two figures in the seats could be seen clearly. Faith, with a collar around her neck, and Eve, dressed in a tight, revealing corset, her arm around Faith.

Faith's stomach churned. This was from the last night she and Eve had gone to Lilith's Den.

On the screen, Eve pushed Faith back against the chair before grabbing her by the collar and planting a forceful kiss on her lips, her hand straying down Faith's chest. A second later, Faith shook her head and cringed away, speaking angrily to Eve. The video had no sound, but Faith's gestures and expression made it clear that things were getting heated. After several seconds, Eve grabbed Faith's hand and dragged her out of frame. The video ended.

Faith cursed under her breath. This did *not* look good. The camera had captured the exact moment when Faith had gotten upset. While in reality, it had been nothing more than a minor quarrel, the distance and the angle of the camera meant that the video showed a very different scene. It looked like Eve was aggressively forcing herself on a somewhat unwilling woman in some kind of dark, perverted sex club. To the outside eye, the scene presented was scandalous. And Eve looked positively predatory.

Faith looked up at Eve. "What's this?"

"Harrison sent it to me," Eve said.

"I don't understand. How did he get this?"

"He took it himself. He was at Lilith's that night. Apparently, a friend of his who's a member let it slip that I go there too. Harrison wanted to see it for himself, so he convinced his friend to take him along as a guest. I don't know if he was trying to catch me in the act or if it was just a coincidence, but he was lucky enough to find me with you. My nanny."

It all clicked together in Faith's mind. Harrison had met her. He knew who Faith was. And now he knew Eve was having some kind of kinky relationship with her nanny.

"What do you think he's going to do with this?" Faith asked.

"I don't have to guess," Eve said. "He told me exactly what he's going to. He's going to use this video as evidence that I'm an unfit mother to bolster his case for custody and have the twins taken from me. That is, unless I comply with his demands."

"He's blackmailing you?"

"He wants me to drop my petition for custody. Let him have the twins full-time. If I do, he'll let me have visitation. If I don't cooperate, he and his lawyers will make sure I'll never get to see the twins again."

"But he can't do that. Not with just this video. It doesn't show you doing anything wrong or illegal."

"No, it doesn't." Eve folded her arms across her chest, holding them tightly to her. "But image matters in the eyes of family court. Good mothers don't go to BDSM clubs or have affairs with their nanny. He's going to use it to paint a picture of me as unstable."

"But that's a lie," Faith said. "And this is just one video. It isn't any evidence of anything."

"He has other evidence. From back when the twins were young. Doctors' reports about my mental state." Eve's voice wavered. "I was in bad shape by the time I went to see a doctor. He can use that."

"That's the ammunition Harrison has against you?" That was why, this entire time, Eve had been determined to be on her best behavior?

Eve nodded. "It's nothing damming, but his lawyers, they'll twist it, make it seem like a bigger deal than it was. Make me seem like a bad mother."

"But that was years ago. And all those problems you had, it was because of him and his messed-up family!"

"I can't blame his family for everything. I'm responsible for the state I was in. I'm responsible for the way I felt."

"No, you're not. Lots of women feel the way you did. It isn't unusual to get depressed after having kids. It doesn't make you a bad mother."

"Not everyone understands that," Eve said. "All a judge is going to see is a mother whose children drove her to despair. Harrison's lawyers will make sure of that. They're the best in the business. Pay them enough, and they can get anyone off for murder. All they have to do is spin me as some kind of mentally ill pervert, and that's it. I lose the twins."

"You have good lawyers too," Faith said. "You can fight this."

"The risks are just too great. If I fight this and I lose, I'll never see the twins again. I can't lose them, Faith."

"So what are you going to do? You can't just give up."

"I don't have a choice! Harrison, he's a powerful man. And he has a never-ending supply of money. I can't go up against him with so much at risk. I can't win against him."

"Yes, you can! You have to try, at least."

"You don't understand." Eve threw her hands up. "How could you? You're not a mother. You don't understand what's at risk here. You couldn't possibly comprehend what this is like."

It was true. Faith didn't know what this felt like. She couldn't imagine the depths of Eve's anguish. "You're right," Faith said. "I'm sorry. I'm sorry this is happening. If there's anything I can do to—"

"No," Eve said. "I called you here to let you know what was going on, but what I need right now is time and space to work this out. The twins will be staying with Harrison until everything is sorted, so they won't be needing a nanny. And I don't need you wrapped up in this mess any further."

"Oh." It was no surprise Eve wanted Faith gone. It was Eve's relationship with her that had caused this, after all. "You're right. It's for the best."

Eve didn't respond. She just continued to stare at nothing at all.

"I'll leave you alone, then." Faith hesitated. "And I'm sorry. I hope you can work things out."

Faith left the room. Eve didn't even look at her. She didn't say goodbye. And as Faith made her way home, Eve's haunted face was all she could see.

CHAPTER TWENTY-THREE

Faith was woken up by the sound of knocking on her front door.

She groaned and threw off her covers, squinting at the sun shining through her curtains. It was almost midday, but she'd spent most of the night a sleepless wreck. She'd only fallen asleep a few hours ago.

The knocking continued. Faith got out of bed and walked out to the door. She opened it up to find Lindsey standing in the hallway.

Crap. "We're supposed to go to lunch," Faith said. "I completely forgot."

"Did you just wake up?" Lindsey asked.

"Yeah. I didn't get much sleep last night."

Lindsey frowned. "Are you okay?"

"You should probably just come in."

Lindsey followed Faith inside. "What's going on?"

"It's Eve." Faith collapsed onto the couch. Lindsey joined her. "Everything is messed up, and it's all my fault." She'd stewed on it overnight. It had made her realize just how bad things were. Eve's family was at risk because of Faith. And now, Eve wanted nothing to do with her.

"What happened?" Lindsey asked.

"What happened is that I ruined everything for her."

"Just tell me what happened. Start from the beginning."

Faith told Lindsey everything, from that night at Lilith's when she'd exploded on Eve, to the moment Eve had shown her the video. Her explanation was all jumbled up, just like the feelings inside her.

"And then she said she needed space and told me not to come back." Faith slumped in her seat. "This is such a mess. Eve is going to lose her kids. All because of me."

"Faith, this isn't your fault," Lindsey said. "I'm sure Eve doesn't blame you for what happened."

"But it *is* my fault. We never should have gotten together in the first place. I was the one who kept pushing her. I had to find out if she was the woman in the corset. I had to confront her when she was being cold to me after the party. I convinced her to continue with this twisted fling of ours, even though we both knew it would put her family at risk. If I'd just let things lie, none of this would have happened."

"You know that's not true. You didn't force Eve into this relationship with you. She made a choice, just like you did."

"Well, clearly she regrets it now," Faith said.

"Are you sure? For starters, did Eve say things were over between you?"

"She didn't have to. She said she needed space. And considering what she's dealing with, that's understandable."

"I'm sure the two of you can work it out," Lindsey said. "Believe me, you don't want things between you to end over a misunderstanding."

"There's no point in trying to work things out. Even if she still wanted to be with me, I wouldn't want to mess things up with her family any further." Faith shook her head. "This is for the best."

"Faith—"

"Really, it is," Faith said. "This is hard. I want to be there for her. I care about her so much. But that's why I have to stay away. You should have seen the look in her eyes." Her shoulders shook in a silent sob. She steadied herself. "I can't risk tearing Eve's family apart. I can't be the reason the twins grow up without a mom."

"Oh, Faith." Lindsey put her hand on Faith's arm. "None of this is your fault. And you haven't torn her family apart. You still don't know how this custody situation is going to turn out."

"Eve doesn't even want to fight it. She's just given up. She thinks the video is the final nail in the coffin."

"Wait." Lindsey cocked her head to the side. "That video. It's from inside Lilith's Den?"

Faith nodded.

"And Eve's ex-husband took it?"

"Yeah."

"You can't take videos inside Lilith's. Didn't you read those agreements you signed the first time you went there?"

"Of course not," Faith said. "There were so many pages!"

"Well, if you'd read them, you'd know that filming inside the club isn't allowed. Even photos aren't allowed. Confidentiality is a big deal there."

"I don't think Harrison cares."

"Maybe he doesn't," Lindsey said. "But he signed those agreements too. Everyone who walks through the doors at

Lilith's Den does. They're legally binding. There are serious penalties for breaching them."

"Penalties? Harrison can just pay his way out of them. Or lawyer his way out of them."

"I don't think so. You know the owner of Lilith's Den? Vanessa? You met her that night I invited you along, remember?"

Faith nodded.

"She'd want to know that this kind of thing happened at her club," Lindsey said. "She takes privacy really seriously. And she might be able to help."

"I doubt she can do anything. I don't think you understand how much money and power Harrison has."

"Vanessa has money and power too. You and Eve should talk to her."

"There's no 'me and Eve,'" Faith said. "Not anymore."

"Well at the very least, you can still tell Eve to talk to Vanessa. Let her know Vanessa might be willing to help." Lindsey frowned. "Now that I think about it, I'm surprised Eve isn't looking into that angle already. If she's a regular at the club, she knows what a big deal it is for someone to take a video inside Lilith's. And on top of that, there's an unwritten rule in the BDSM community that you don't out anyone. *Ever.*"

Eve had said the same thing to Faith once. "I guess she didn't think of that. This whole situation has her really shaken up."

"All the more reason you should talk to her about it," Lindsey said.

"She made it clear that she didn't want to see me." Eve was right to feel that way.

An exasperated look crossed Lindsey's face. "Just think about it, okay? Right now, you're hurting. Eve isn't the only one who isn't seeing things clearly. Promise me you'll take some time to think it over?"

"Fine," Faith muttered.

"Good." Lindsey placed her hands on Faith's shoulders. "You can't give up on her, Faith. What you have with her, it's something special. I don't even know her, but I can tell. You've been different lately. Happier. More like the Faith I met our first day of art school."

"Is that a good thing?" Back then, Faith had been newly eighteen and still adjusting to the real world after years of being caged. She'd gone a little wild.

Lindsey smiled. "I think it is."

Faith sighed. The years that had followed had been tumultuous, but she'd felt freer than ever before. And Eve had given her back that feeling.

But that was all over now. She'd screwed everything up for Eve. Eve was right to get rid of her. Right to ask for space.

It was better if she just stayed away.

CHAPTER TWENTY-FOUR

Faith lay on her old gray couch, staring up at the ceiling. She had nothing to do now that she was out of a job. Sure, Eve hadn't explicitly fired her. But she'd made it clear she didn't need Faith's services. And she'd made it clear she wanted nothing to do with Faith.

Faith hugged a cushion to her chest. Several days had passed since that night in Eve's office, and she'd been consumed by worry ever since. It wasn't just Eve she was worried about. What was going to happen to the twins if Eve gave up fighting for them?

Faith didn't know much about Harrison and his family other than what Eve had told her. They'd certainly made Eve's life hell. But that didn't mean they would treat the twins the same way. Leah and Ethan had never had anything bad to say about their father and grandparents. Maybe living with them full-time wouldn't be so bad for the twins.

Faith threw the cushion across the room. She was deluding herself. There was only one thing about the situation that Faith was certain of. Eve was a good mother. She was a good person.

She didn't deserve to lose her kids.

Lindsey's advice played in her head again. Faith had a potential solution to Eve's problem in her lap. Didn't she owe it to Eve to tell her? It was a solution Eve couldn't see for herself. She was too scared. She wasn't thinking straight. She was giving up when she could still fight.

Faith sighed. Wasn't she doing the exact same thing Eve was? Letting fear win? Wasn't that why she was so adamant that she had to stay away from Eve? She kept telling herself that Eve wanted her gone, but that wasn't what was truly keeping her away. She'd shut herself off from even the idea of ever seeing Eve again, not for Eve's sake, but for her own. She'd fled at the first sign of rejection, just to keep herself from feeling that same pain she'd felt so many times before.

Faith steeled herself. This wasn't about her, or her feelings. This was about Eve and keeping her family together. Faith owed it to Eve to help her in any way she could.

She just hoped Eve would listen.

Faith rang Eve's doorbell and waited. She didn't even know if Eve was home. She still had a key, but she wasn't about to waltz into the house after everything that had happened.

She glanced at the camera by the doorbell. Had Eve seen her already? Was she ignoring her, waiting for Faith to give up and leave? Faith wouldn't blame her. If she was in Eve's shoes, she wouldn't want to see Faith either.

She was about to leave when the door swung open.

"Hello, Faith," Eve said.

Faith's heart sank. Eve looked as put together as ever, but her face was a mask of worry. It hurt to see her like this. Faith longed to wrap her arms around her, tell her everything was going to be okay. But it wasn't her place. And that wasn't why she was here.

She pulled herself together. She had to focus on helping Eve.

Eve stepped to the side. "Why don't you come in?"

Faith followed Eve through the house and into the living room. There was no sign of the twins. Eve sat down stiffly on the couch. Faith joined her.

Eve looked at Faith, her eyes filled with emotion, and gave her a faint smile. "It's good to see you."

Why was Eve smiling at her? Why, when she was in the midst of this crisis, caused by Faith herself?

Faith's resolve crumbled under Eve's gaze. "I'm sorry," she blurted out. "I'm so sorry, and I know you don't want to see me again, but I want to help you. I want to fix this, and I think I know how."

"Faith." Eve held up her hands. "Slow down. What are you talking about?"

"I caused this whole mess, and you said you wanted space, but I need to tell you how you can fix all this."

"What? You didn't cause this. And when I said I needed space, I meant space to think." Realization dawned on Eve's face. "Did you think I meant I didn't want to see you again?"

"Well, yeah."

Eve flinched back. "I didn't mean that. I didn't mean to come across as so cold. I was distracted, worried about losing the twins, and I didn't think about what I was saying. I never meant for you to think this was your fault."

Had Faith really misread everything? For some reason, the knowledge didn't make her feel any better.

"I know I said some harsh things, and I'm sorry," Eve said. "I shouldn't have pushed you away. I shouldn't have said you wouldn't understand because you're not a mother. And I shouldn't have said I needed space. I regret saying that so much. Faith, this whole time, I've been beside myself with worry. I wanted so badly for you to be here with me. But I thought that you'd want space too." Her eyes wavered. "I dragged you into this family drama that you should never have been involved in. I didn't think you'd want to be a part of that."

"I thought that was what you wanted," Faith said. "Me, out of the way."

"I would never, ever want that. Faith, the other night I said that what we have has made me feel more alive than I ever have in years. More complete." She laid her hand on top of Faith's on the couch between them. "I didn't mean having you as my submissive. I meant how I feel about you in my heart. I care about you, Faith. I want to be with you."

Something flitted inside Faith's chest. Wasn't that what Faith wanted too?

But she had too many conflicting feelings swirling about inside her. Too many doubts, too many uncertainties. And she couldn't possibly be happy with Eve knowing that their relationship was destroying Eve's family.

She drew her hand away. None of that mattered right now. She had to tell Eve how she could fix things.

"That's not why I came here," Faith said. "I came to tell

you that I have an idea of how to handle the situation with Harrison."

A pained expression crossed Eve's face, but it quickly disappeared. "All right. Tell me."

Faith took a breath and explained what Lindsey had told her. About Harrison breaching the club's agreement and how they could use it to fight him.

"So," Faith said. "What do you think?"

Eve sat forward, leaning toward Faith. "You're right. I hadn't thought about any of that. But I don't know if it will help. I don't know if there's anything we can do about it, even with Vanessa's help."

"I don't know either," Faith said. "But you have to try. Eve, I've gotten to know your family so well since I started working for you. I care about you, and I care about the twins. I know as well as you do that Harrison getting full custody isn't the best thing for them. I know that splitting your family apart like this isn't right. You have to fight this. If not for your sake, then for Leah and Ethan's."

"You're right," Eve said. "God, you're right. The more I think about it, the more I'm certain that I can't let this happen. I can't let the twins be taken in by the kind of people that would do something like this. By the kind of man who would blackmail the mother of his children." Her jaw set. "I can't let him do this."

"So you're going to fight this?"

Eve nodded. "Let's call Vanessa."

CHAPTER TWENTY-FIVE

*E*ve drummed her fingers on the tabletop. She and Faith were in the conference room at Eve's office, waiting for Harrison to arrive. The trap was set. However, one crucial piece of the plan was missing.

Faith looked at Eve. Her face was wrinkled with worry. She took Eve's hand under the table and squeezed it. "Don't worry," she said. "She'll be here. This is going to work." It had to. The fate of Eve's family all depended on it. "Everything will be okay."

Eve gave her a half-smile. "Thanks again for agreeing to come along. I really appreciate it."

"I meant it when I said that I'm here for you if you need me." Faith still hadn't made up her mind about the two of them, but she couldn't bear to see Eve like this.

The door swung open. A tall, raven-haired woman strode into the room. "Sorry I'm late," Vanessa said. "I got held up in traffic."

"It's fine," Eve said. "Harrison isn't here yet."

Eve had called her ex-husband the day before and asked

him to meet her here to discuss the custody situation. She'd made it sound like she was ready to give in to his demands. He'd made her promise not to bring her lawyers.

He hadn't mentioned bringing anyone else along.

"Faith." Vanessa nodded at her. "Hello again."

"Hi." Faith was surprised that Vanessa remembered her. They'd only met once, at Lilith's Den that night. It seemed like so long ago. "Thanks for helping out with this."

"It's no trouble." Vanessa sat down at the end of the table. "Besides, it's in my best interests to resolve this. No one violates the privacy of my club and gets away with it. And I won't stand for this kind of disgusting blackmail."

Although Vanessa appeared calm and collected, the anger in her voice was palpable. That was reassuring. She really seemed to care about the situation. Faith sensed Eve relax a little too.

The door to the conference room opened again. In walked Harrison with that same confident swagger he'd shown the last time Faith had met him.

He looked around the room, his eyes clouding over. "I told you to meet me alone."

"You said no lawyers," Eve said. "You didn't say anything about anyone else."

Harrison's eyes landed on Faith. He snorted. "You brought your nanny? The one you're fucking?"

"She's not just my nanny," Eve said. "She's so much more to me than that. And I brought her along for support."

He looked between the two of them. "So this is the real reason you left me? Because you're a lesbian?"

"Oh, please. Leaving you had nothing to do with my sexuality."

Vanessa cleared her throat. "Are you two done? We have more important things to discuss."

Harrison looked at Vanessa, frowning. "I know you from somewhere."

"Vanessa Harper," she said.

Recognition dawned on his face. Apparently, on top of secretly owning Lilith's Den, Vanessa was some big-shot CEO. Her power and status were what their whole plan hinged on. It was clear from Harrison's reaction that her name held a lot of weight.

"What are you doing here?" Harrison asked.

Vanessa gestured toward a chair across from Eve and Faith. "Why don't you have a seat?"

Harrison sat down, a bemused expression on his face.

"Eve and I are acquaintances," Vanessa continued. "She told me all about you and your little blackmail plot. You see, you probably don't know this about me, but I own Lilith's Den."

Harrison's face twisted with disgust. "You own that fucked-up place?"

"I do. And that 'fucked-up place' is patronized by lots of powerful people. They all take their privacy very seriously, for obvious reasons. It's why the club has such strict confidentiality rules. By taking a video inside the club, you violated those rules."

Harrison crossed his arms. "So, I broke some rules. It's too late to do anything about it now. You can ban me if you like. I'm never going back there."

"Oh, I can do much more than ban you." Vanessa's voice grew icy. "Before you entered Lilith's Den, you signed a number of legally binding agreements. One of these was a confidentiality agreement, which included a clause prohibiting any photography or recording of videos inside the premises."

"What, you're going to sue me?" Harrison said. "You know as well as I do that we'll just end up in a drawn-out legal battle. Are you sure you'll come out on top?"

"I have no doubt I'd win such a case. My legal team created those agreements to be ironclad. But no, I'm not threatening to sue you. I could do that. But I could do much, much worse." Vanessa leaned back in her chair. "We have a lot of mutual friends, you and I. Colleagues. Business contacts. Given your distaste for what goes on in my club, you may be shocked to hear that many of our mutual contacts are regulars at Lilith's Den."

Harrison tensed. Could he see where this was going?

"All those regulars are very private about the fact that they go to my club. And for a good reason, when there are judgmental people like you out there who are willing to expose what they like to do behind closed doors. How do you think they'd react if they knew you'd entered their sanctuary and taken a video in order to blackmail someone?"

"I wouldn't do that to anyone else," Harrison said. "Eve is my ex-wife. The mother of my children. It's different."

"Is it? And how does anyone else know you wouldn't do the same thing to them? Why would anyone ever trust you again, knowing you violated such an important social contract? Knowing how little respect you have for their privacy? You know how the corporate world works. It's all about building relationships. Building trust. Why would anyone want to do business with someone who has proven they can't be trusted?"

"Are you saying you'll have me blacklisted?"

"I would never do anything as unsubtle as that," Vanessa said. "But the patrons of my club will want to know that their confidentiality has been violated, and by whom. When word gets around, you'll lose all your contracts, one by one. Do you think your company can survive that?"

Harrison looked at Vanessa, wide-eyed. "You're talking about sabotaging my company."

"I wouldn't be sabotaging anything. I'd simply be informing people of the facts and letting nature take its course. Of course, you have enough money that you'd be fine, even without your company. But what would that do to your reputation? You'll be ruined, just like you threatened to ruin Eve here."

"You're crazy." Harrison shook his head. "What do you want from me?"

"What do you think?" Vanessa narrowed her eyes. "I want you to wipe that video and any others you took inside Lilith's Den from the face of the earth. And I want you to give Eve whatever she asks for when it comes to this custody case."

"You don't know anything about that. About my family, about Eve."

"I know enough. I know that you're the kind of man who tries to blackmail his ex-wife, and that speaks volumes. My fiancée is a lawyer. She's informed me that judges don't look kindly upon people who blackmail their former spouses in custody cases. It's in your best interests to cooperate with Eve."

Harrison scoffed and turned to Eve. "Isn't this what you're doing to me? Blackmailing me, having *her* threaten me unless I agree to your demands?"

Eve shrugged. "You stopped playing by the rules a long time ago. I'm just leveling the playing field." She crossed her arms. "They're my children, Harrison. I'm willing to do anything for them. And I mean *anything*."

"If you cared about the kids you wouldn't be having an affair with their nanny and going to sex clubs. You're their mother for god's sake."

"Yes, I'm the twins' mother. But I'm a person too, with needs of my own, which is something you never understood. I'm allowed to have a life outside of my children. I'm allowed to find my own happiness."

"Happiness?" Harrison looked at Faith. "With their nanny? You're exposing the twins to this sick fetish of yours."

"I'm not exposing them to anything. They don't know about Faith and me, and I intend to keep things that way. What I do in my spare time is none of their business, or yours. Faith and I are both consenting adults. There is nothing sick about what's between us." Eve's jaw set. "What I have with Faith is more real than anything I've ever felt. I love her."

What? Faith looked at Eve. Her eyes were locked onto Harrison's, but the resolve on her face made it clear that she meant every word she'd said.

"This is crazy." Harrison threw his hands up. "If you think I'm going to roll over and give you whatever you want, you're out of your mind."

"I don't think you have a choice," Vanessa interrupted.

"Not unless you want to lose your company." Vanessa's eyes bored into him. "This isn't an empty threat. Release that video and I will ruin you."

Faith stared at Vanessa in shock. She was serious, and Harrison knew it.

"Delete the video," Vanessa said. "Work things out with Eve. And if I hear of you doing anything less, I will let you and your company burn."

Harrison spoke through gritted teeth. "Fine."

"And I'm going to need the name of this friend of yours who invited you to Lilith's Den."

Harrison muttered a name.

"Good. I'm going to have a word with him about his choice of guests." Vanessa stood up. "We'll let the two of you talk. Faith?"

Faith got up. "Good luck," she said quietly to Eve.

Eve nodded. "Wait for me in my office. This won't take long."

Faith followed Vanessa out of the room and shut the door. She was dizzy with nerves.

Vanessa put her hand on Faith's shoulder. "Don't worry. Everything is going to be fine. I do my fair share of negotiating, and I can tell when someone is on their back. Harrison will give Eve whatever she wants."

"I hope so," Faith said. "Thanks for all your help."

"Once again, it's no trouble." Vanessa paused. "Eve told me about the two of you. How everything started when you ran into each other at Lilith's Den. I'm glad my club played a part in bringing two people together. That's what life's all about isn't it?"

"Yeah," Faith said. "Thanks again."

"I have to go. Let me know if Eve has any trouble, okay?"

"I will."

Vanessa strode off. Faith went to Eve's office and sat down in front of the desk. Several minutes passed. She got up. She was too nervous to sit still. She paced in front of the window. Eve was taking forever.

Faith hoped for Eve's sake that this worked. She cared so much for the beautiful family she'd spent so long getting to know. And she cared so much for Eve.

Eve's words echoed in her mind. *What I have with Faith is more real than anything I've ever felt.*

I love her.

"Faith."

She turned. She hadn't heard Eve walk in. "How did it go?"

Eve joined her by the window. "Harrison is going to delete the video. And we came to an agreement. He's giving me primary custody of Leah and Ethan."

Faith's heart swelled. "That's great!"

"We're still working out the finer details, and none of this is official until we get our lawyers to sign off on everything. But Harrison seems remorseful. He seems to genuinely want to work with me. I considered pushing for sole custody, but whether I like it or not, Harrison is the twins' father. Despite his many, many flaws, he deserves a hand in raising them. I'll just have to be extra careful that his family's values don't rub off on the twins. I'll have to set the best example I can and hope that it's enough."

"It will be," Faith said. "You're an incredible mother. Leah and Ethan are going to grow up just fine. I'm so happy for you all. I'm so glad you fought this."

"You were right all along. I should have listened to you. I was just scared."

"With so much at stake, you had a good reason to be scared. And once again, sorry for my part in this."

Eve gave her a hard look. "Faith, if you apologize one more time…"

"Sorry! I'll stop. I'm just glad everything is sorted out now."

"No. Everything isn't sorted out." Eve's eyes locked onto Faith's. "There's still the matter of us."

The air in the room grew still.

"There's nothing standing in our way anymore," Eve said. "Nothing stopping us from being together."

It was true. There were no more obstacles in their way. No reason for them to hide. Nothing stopping them from embracing what they felt.

Nothing stopping Faith from surrendering to what she truly felt for Eve.

Faith took a step toward Eve, and another, until they were barely a foot apart. "You said something in there. You said that you love me."

"Did I?" A slight smile crossed Eve's lips. "It must have slipped out. But it's the truth."

Eve took Faith's hand, closing the distance between them.

"I love you, Faith."

With those four words, all Faith's doubts melted away. "I love you too."

Eve swept Faith into her arms for a heady kiss that almost knocked Faith off her feet.

CHAPTER TWENTY-SIX

Faith stood in the living room door, watching Eve recline on the lounge with a book. Eve, spending the evening relaxing? That was a sight Faith never thought she'd see.

Eve looked up at Faith. "You're back. The kids are at Harrison's?"

Faith nodded. She'd just dropped them off. The new custody agreement had been in place for a few weeks now, and it was working well. Eve was much more relaxed these days. And Faith finally had a regular work schedule now that the twins had a set routine. However, she ended up spending most of her days off with Eve anyway.

It was a relief, to finally be able to be with Eve openly. However, they still hadn't told the twins about their relationship. They were taking things slow on that front. Whenever the twins were home, Faith and Eve continued to keep things strictly professional between them.

But right now, they had the house all to themselves.

"And you've tidied up the kids' rooms?" Eve asked. "Folded their laundry? Packed away their toys?"

"Everything is taken care of," Faith said.

"Good. I have one last task for you."

"What do you need me to do for you?"

Eve placed her book down carefully and stood up. "I need you to go wait for me in my bedroom." The look in her eyes made it abundantly clear that this task had nothing to do with Faith's job.

Faith chewed her lip, feigning hesitation. "I don't know. I'm supposed to be off the clock."

Eve grabbed Faith's arm and yanked her in close. Faith yelped in surprise.

Eve spoke into her ear in a sharp voice. "Consider this overtime." She released Faith from her grasp. "You have five minutes. When I come in, I expect to find you kneeling on the bed." She ran her eyes down Faith's body. "And take that dress off."

Faith gave her a cheeky grin. "You're the boss."

She headed to Eve's bedroom, closed the door, and stripped off her dress before climbing onto the vast bed, kneeling in the center of it. At least Eve had asked Faith to kneel on the bed and not on the floor like she had a few times before. Now that she and Eve were free of all the restrictions that came with a secret relationship, Eve had gotten far more creative with her games. She seemed to revel in coming up with delightful new ways to torment Faith. Just thinking about it made her ache.

After what seemed like an eternity, Eve entered the room. Faith's lips fell open. In that short space of time, Eve had undergone a transformation. Her hair was loose, and her lips were a dark crimson that made Faith want to taste them. And the rest of her? Faith didn't know where to look. The red-soled heels Eve wore elongated her smooth, bare legs, and the tiniest pair of black panties were on her hips. The only other piece of clothing Eve had on was a black corset. It was the same corset she'd worn to Lilith's the first night Faith had set foot inside.

Seeing Eve dressed in that outfit flooded every cell in Faith's body with need. And yet, the woman who stood before Faith was so far removed from the woman in the corset from that night. She wasn't the Eve that Faith had met the day of her job interview either. Although she was just as strict and domineering, the fire behind her eyes spoke of both passion and warmth. This Eve, Faith's Eve, was far more irresistible than the woman in the corset.

Eve's eyes wandered down Faith's near-naked kneeling form. She hadn't swapped her glasses out for contact lenses like she often did, and the way she gazed at Faith from over the top of them sent Faith's pulse racing.

Faith peered back up at her from under her eyelashes. "Do you like what you see?"

Eve grabbed Faith's chin, jerking it toward her. "You're being far too cheeky today. For the rest of the night, you're not to speak unless spoken to. Do you understand?"

Faith nodded. Pushing the limits of the woman who held Faith's pleasure in her hand was *not* a smart idea.

"For the record, I do like what I see," Eve said. "I always do."

Eve leaned down to kiss her, pressing herself against Faith so forcefully that they both tumbled onto the bed. Eve tore off Faith's bra and panties, her lips never leaving

Faith's. Faith deepened the kiss, the fire within her flickering and flaring.

Eve drew back and reached over the side of the bed to open one of the drawers underneath it. It was already unlocked. Eve was prepared. What did she have planned?

Eve dug around in the drawer, then pulled out the spreader bar. She dropped it on the bed by Faith's feet. "I'll need your ankles."

Faith sat back, her legs stretched out before her, memories of that night on camera flooding her mind and body.

"Not like that," Eve said. "I want you on all fours. And turn around."

Heat rushed to Faith's skin. A position like that, combined with the spreader bar, would leave Faith vulnerable. But she trusted Eve. And that was what made it so delicious.

Faith got on her hands and knees, facing the headboard.

"That's better." Eve picked up the spreader bar and disappeared behind her.

Faith turned her head to watch. Eve pushed Faith's knees apart and fastened the cuffs of the bar around her ankles, leaving her legs spread out. Her thighs burned from the strain, but not in an unpleasant way.

"There." Eve's eyes met Faith's. "You just can't help but peek, can you? I'll have to do something about that." She leaned over, reached into the drawer under the bed again, and produced a long piece of black fabric. "Close your eyes."

Faith opened her mouth to protest. Eve hadn't told her not to look. It wasn't fair of her to make up the rules as she went along. But Eve had instructed Faith not to speak, so she clamped her mouth shut and closed her eyes.

Eve tied the blindfold around Faith's head. Here she was, her ass sticking out, unable to move her legs, unable to see a thing. This was going to be agonizing. Eve had a sadistic streak, but her tool of choice wasn't pain. It was pure, concentrated pleasure. She wielded it like a weapon, sometimes doling it out in agonizingly small slivers, sometimes assaulting Faith with it until she begged for release. Faith already knew that wouldn't take long. Just kneeling on the bed, waiting for Eve, had her hot all over. Not to mention, soaking wet.

The bed shifted under her as Eve got up from it and opened another drawer. Faith waited patiently, powerless to see or do anything. She rolled her shoulders just to remind herself that she could still move.

Finally, Eve returned to the bed, the unexpected motion of the mattress nearly throwing Faith off-balance. Without her sight, she had no frame of reference for anything. It was dizzying.

"All this, and you haven't spoken a single word?" Eve drew the back of her fingers down Faith's cheek and neck. "I thought you would have cracked by now."

Faith said nothing. Eve let her fingers skim between Faith's shoulder blades, along the concave curve of her back, all the way to her tailbone. Faith quivered with delight. The blindfold made all her other senses heightened.

Out of nowhere, Eve slid a finger between Faith's lower lips. Faith gasped. Eve's other hand crept up the back of Faith's thigh, then forward to cup her breasts.

Faith kneeled there, held in place by the spreader bar, as Eve worked her body with a familiarity unlike anything else. She traced the pads of her fingers over the sensitive spot on Faith's neck that made her shiver, teased her nipples with the lightest of touches until they hardened into peaks, scratched her fingernails along Faith's skin, leaving stinging trails behind. With her other hand, she painted swirls around Faith's nub and glided her fingers over Faith's entrance in a way that was equal parts pleasurable and maddening. Faith sank into the darkness, letting Eve and all the sweet sensations Eve lavished her with wash over her.

She let out a strangled breath, her pleasure rising.

"Already?" Eve's honeyed voice was right next to Faith's ear. "I'm nowhere near done with you yet. If I let you come now, you'll have to come for me again, okay?"

Faith whimpered. "Yes." She didn't even know if that was even possible for her, but she was so desperate for release.

"You don't sound convinced." Eve planted a sharp slap on Faith's ass cheek, inflaming her even more. "If I say you'll come, you'll come. Your body belongs to me. Your mind belongs to me. Your pleasure belongs to me."

Faith shuddered. "Yes, Eve. I'm yours."

Suddenly, she felt something warm and wet against her folds, trailing down to her clit. Eve's tongue. Faith let out a moan, her arms almost buckling.

Eve grabbed on to Faith's ass cheeks, devouring her. It took only seconds before Faith reached the edge. A soundless cry erupted in her chest, her fingers gripping the sheets as an earth-shattering orgasm rocked her.

Eve eased off, brushing her lips between Faith's legs with the gentlest of touches. Even so, it was too intense for her sensitized bud. She hissed through her teeth but resisted the urge to edge away. And as Eve caressed Faith's body, her touch began to feel good again.

A soft murmur spilled from Faith's lips. The ache at the peak of her thighs had gone from satisfied to hollow.

"You see?" Eve took hold of Faith's hips. "You should have a little more faith in your Mistress's talents. I'm going to unravel you again in no time."

The bed rocked again. A moment later, something pressed against Faith's lower lips. It wasn't Eve's fingers. Not only was it more solid, but Eve's hands were firmly clutching Faith's hips.

Anticipation welled up inside her. Eve was wearing a strap-on.

Eve drew the tip of the strap-on up and down Faith's slit, rolling it over her clit. Faintly, Faith could feel vibrations emanating from it. They ramped up, resonating deep into her. She bit the inside of her cheek, trying to distract herself from the throbbing inside, waiting for Eve to give her what she craved.

Instead, Eve pulled away and flipped Faith onto her back, propping her up against the pillows and pushing the spreader bar up so that Faith's feet were in the air. With the blindfold on, Eve's rough movements were disorienting.

Before Faith had a chance to regain her bearings, she felt the tip of the strap-on against her once more. With the spreader bar keeping her legs forced apart, all it would take was one push for Eve to be inside her.

Faith drew in a long breath. Slowly, Eve buried herself deep, filling Faith completely. A groan rose from her chest, her body loosening. She grabbed on to the pillow above her head with one hand, the other reaching up to pull Eve closer to her. Eve pierced her over and over to a steady rhythm, the vibrations shooting straight into her core. She rolled her hips back against Eve, her restrained legs trying vainly to clench around the other woman's waist.

In the darkness, Faith felt Eve's cheek press against hers. She clutched blindly at Eve's neck, holding on against the tide of sensations that threatened to sweep her away, chanting Eve's name as she came closer and closer to oblivion.

"Oh, Eve!" Ecstasy surged through her, overwhelming all her senses. She threw her head back, arching up into Eve. At the same time, Eve trembled atop her in an orgasm that mirrored Faith's. Despite the tremors going through her, Faith kept rocking in time with Eve, drawing out both their pleasure.

As they came back down to earth together, Eve smothered Faith's lips with her own in an endless kiss. Faith had fallen into that heavenly trance that only Eve seemed to be able to bring about in her.

Eve crawled down the bed to remove the spreader bar from Faith's ankles before kissing her way back up Faith's body.

"Don't think for a second that I'm done with you," Eve said. "I plan to take full advantage of the fact that we have the house to ourselves for the night." She stroked a hand down Faith's hair, letting her fingers trail over the blindfold. "And don't think I missed your slip up just now. You said my name, didn't you?"

Faith nodded, remembering Eve's command for silence far too late.

"I'm feeling generous." Eve drew Faith in close. "I'll let you have a few minutes before dealing with your little lapse. My riding crop could use a workout."

Faith sank into the other woman's arms and let out a blissful sigh. She was in for a long night. She couldn't think of anything she'd rather be doing with Eve.

She understood it now, what everything between them was about. There was a kind of freedom in submission. A power in embracing her vulnerability. A sweetness that came with surrendering to Eve, and an intimacy unlike anything else.

Eve removed the blindfold from Faith's eyes, but Faith didn't open them. The stillness between her and Eve was too precious to disturb.

EPILOGUE

EVE

2 years later

Eve looked at the clock on the living room wall. Faith was due to arrive any minute now. The stage was set. The guests had arrived. All that was missing was the woman of the hour.

Down the hall, the front door opened. Faith and Lindsey's voices echoed through the house. The two of them had been out all day on a shopping trip to celebrate Faith's birthday. In reality, it was an excuse to get Faith out of the house so Eve could prepare for the night. As far as Faith knew, she and Eve were having a simple birthday dinner at home with Lindsey and Camilla. She had no idea that Eve had bigger plans.

"Eve?" Faith called down the hall. "I'm home."

"They're probably in the living room," Lindsey said innocently.

Faith and Lindsey's footsteps grew closer and closer, then stopped at the door.

"Let me get that for you," Lindsey said. A moment later, she slid the door to the living room open.

Two dozen voices rang out at once. "Happy Birthday!"

Faith's hand flew up to her chest. She stared wide-eyed around the room, scanning the faces looking back at her. Her eyes landed on Eve. "What's going on?"

"What do you think?" Eve said. "It's a surprise party."

Faith's mouth fell open. "How did you do everything without me noticing? How long have you been planning this?"

"Just a few months. Lindsey helped."

Faith glared at Lindsey, her hands on her hips. "So that's why you've been acting weird all day. I can't believe you kept this from me. Both of you."

"It wasn't easy," Eve said. "But it was worth it to see the look on your face just now."

"This is amazing." Faith looked around the room again. "There are so many people here."

Eve had sent out the invitations weeks earlier, and almost everyone she'd invited had shown up. There were a handful of Faith's classmates from college, and a few other people Lindsey had invited. Eve and Faith's mutual friends, including Lindsey and Camilla, Vanessa and her wife, and all the others they'd grown close to over the years. Vicki, the woman who had introduced Eve to Lilith's Den all these years ago, was here too, along with her girlfriend, although Vicki was no longer the womanizing playgirl she'd once been, having settled down long ago.

This was Faith's family now, all these people who loved her. It warmed Eve's heart that Faith had finally found that family she'd been so desperately searching for.

"Hannah?" Faith spotted her aunt, her eyes growing wide. "You're here."

Faith ran over to Hannah and threw her arms around her. It had been a long time since she and her aunt had last seen each other in person, so Eve had flown Hannah to the city just for the occasion. As for the rest of Faith's family, Faith never heard from her sister or anyone else again, but Hannah kept an eye on them and let Faith know they were okay now and then.

With the guest of honor in attendance, the party ramped up. As Faith greeted everyone, Eve helped herself to a drink and took a seat. It would take Faith a while to catch up with all her friends. Eve watched her bounce around the room. They'd both come a long way since that day Faith had turned up at Eve's house years ago.

It was Faith's house now too, although that was only a recent development. With the twins involved, she and Eve hadn't wanted to rush into anything. The fact that Eve kept Faith on as their nanny didn't make things easy. For the longest time, they'd hidden their relationship from the twins. It was the responsible thing to do. But as Leah and Ethan had grown older, it had become impossible for Eve and Faith to keep anything from them.

Fortunately, the twins were fully on board with the relationship. They loved Faith. Since Faith practically lived at the house anyway, it only made sense that she move in. It had been a bit of an adjustment, but Faith was a part of the family now. They hadn't made anything official. Faith was wary of marriage, given her history, and Eve wasn't in a rush to get married again. However, Eve fully intended to make Faith hers in her own way.

Lindsey and Camilla spotted Eve and came to sit down next to her.

"Thanks for your help today, Lindsey," Eve said. "I trust that keeping Faith occupied all day wasn't too difficult?"

"It was a breeze," Lindsey replied. "Although she did start to get suspicious in the afternoon. I had to distract her by asking her to be my maid of honor."

"I bet that worked like a charm," Eve said.

For someone who didn't want to get married, Faith sure liked weddings. When Lindsey and Camilla had announced their engagement a few months back, Faith had been giddy with excitement. But Faith had always been a contradiction of a woman, and Eve knew that, despite her experiences, Faith was a romantic at heart.

"Does that mean you've finally started planning the wedding?" Eve asked.

"Barely," Camilla said. "There's just so much to do."

Lindsey rolled her eyes. "Camilla is such a perfectionist. At this rate, the wedding is still years away."

"Now, everything worth doing is worth doing properly," Camilla said. "Speaking of weddings, I need to ask Vanessa who she used as her planner. They had such a lovely ceremony, don't you think?"

Camilla spotted Vanessa nearby and waved to her. Vanessa grabbed her wife's hand and drew her over to where Eve, Camilla, and Lindsey sat. Soon, they were deep in conversation about wedding planning. Eve excused herself and went to find Faith.

It was another hour before Faith and Eve were able to have a moment alone. Still brimming with excitement, Faith took Eve's hand and pulled her out into the hall. The sounds of the party faded.

"Thanks for all this, Eve," Faith said. "This is the best birthday present I could have ever asked for."

"It's my pleasure," Eve said. "And the party isn't the only present I have for you." She held out a small box. "Here. Open it."

Faith's face lit up. She took the box from Eve, untied the ribbon, and opened it up. Inside was a silver eternity ring with rubies and emeralds all around the band. It was flashier than anything Eve would wear, but it suited Faith's out-there style.

"It's a ring," Faith said.

"It's not just a ring. It's a promise." Eve took Faith's hand. "I know how you feel about marriage, but I wanted to give you something that says you're mine. Something that says I'll be here for you no matter what. Something that says forever."

"Eve." Faith eyes sparkled brighter than the ring. "It's beautiful. I love it." She wrapped her arms around Eve's neck, drawing her into an embrace. "And just so you know, I've been reconsidering how I feel about marriage. With everyone around us getting married, all this wedding stuff, it's kind of sweet. I still don't know if I want to get married myself, but who knows? Maybe one day that will change."

Eve smiled. "Either way, there's one thing that will never change, and that's the way I feel about you. I know I want to spend the rest of my life with you, and that's all that matters."

Eve kissed her softly, then took the ring out of the box and slipped it on Faith's finger.

It was a perfect fit.

ABOUT THE AUTHOR

Anna Stone is the bestselling author of Being Hers. Her lesbian romance novels are sweet, passionate, and sizzle with heat. When she isn't writing, Anna can usually be found relaxing on the beach with a book.
Anna currently lives on the sunny east coast of Australia.

Visit www.annastoneauthor.com for information on her books and to sign up for her newsletter.

facebook.com/AnnaStoneRomance
twitter.com/AnnaStoneAuthor

Printed in Great Britain
by Amazon

Freeing HER

Faith is thrilled to land a job as a nanny for a wealthy, recently divorced mother of two. The pay is great, and the kids are angels. The only problem is their mother, Eve. She's uptight, controlling, and impossible to please. The worst part? Faith can't stop thinking about her.

When Faith discovers a side to her new boss that she never expected, it becomes clear that behind Eve's strict facade is a passionate woman bursting to break free and make Faith hers. Faith knows all too well what it's like to keep part of herself hidden. And she finds Eve and the sweet surrender she demands irresistible.

But as they confront their long-suppressed desires, Eve and Faith must keep everything between them secret or they risk losing everything. Eve is locked in a custody battle with her ex-husband, and he isn't afraid to play dirty. As the stakes rise and fear threatens to drive them apart, will Faith and Eve find the strength to stand together?

ISBN 9780648419259